Conquer

Omega Queen Series, Volume 4

W.J. May

Published by Dark Shadow Publishing, 2020.

This is a work of fiction. Similarities to real people, places, or events are entirely coincidental.

CONQUER

First edition. May 10, 2020.

Copyright © 2020 W.J. May.

Written by W.J. May.

Also by W.J. May

Bit-Lit Series
Lost Vampire
Cost of Blood
Price of Death

Blood Red Series
Courage Runs Red
The Night Watch
Marked by Courage
Forever Night
The Other Side of Fear
Blood Red Box Set Books #1-5

Daughters of Darkness: Victoria's Journey
Victoria
Huntress
Coveted (A Vampire & Paranormal Romance)
Twisted
Daughter of Darkness - Victoria - Box Set

Great Temptation Series
The Devil's Footsteps
Heaven's Command
Mortals Surrender

Hidden Secrets Saga
Seventh Mark - Part 1
Seventh Mark - Part 2
Marked By Destiny
Compelled
Fate's Intervention
Chosen Three
The Hidden Secrets Saga: The Complete Series

Kerrigan Chronicles
Stopping Time
A Passage of Time
Ticking Clock
Secrets in Time
Time in the City
Ultimate Future

Mending Magic Series
Lost Souls
Illusion of Power
Challenging the Dark

Castle of Power
Limits of Magic
Protectors of Light

Omega Queen Series
Discipline
Bravery
Courage
Conquer

Paranormal Huntress Series
Never Look Back
Coven Master
Alpha's Permission
Blood Bonding
Oracle of Nightmares
Shadows in the Night
Paranormal Huntress BOX SET #1-3

Prophecy Series
Only the Beginning
White Winter
Secrets of Destiny

Royal Factions
The Price For Peace

The Cost for Surviving

The Chronicles of Kerrigan
Rae of Hope
Dark Nebula
House of Cards
Royal Tea
Under Fire
End in Sight
Hidden Darkness
Twisted Together
Mark of Fate
Strength & Power
Last One Standing
Rae of Light
The Chronicles of Kerrigan Box Set Books # 1 - 6

The Chronicles of Kerrigan: Gabriel
Living in the Past
Present For Today
Staring at the Future

The Chronicles of Kerrigan Prequel
Christmas Before the Magic
Question the Darkness
Into the Darkness
Fight the Darkness
Alone in the Darkness

Lost in Darkness
The Chronicles of Kerrigan Prequel Series Books #1-3

The Chronicles of Kerrigan Sequel
A Matter of Time
Time Piece
Second Chance
Glitch in Time
Our Time
Precious Time

The Hidden Secrets Saga
Seventh Mark (part 1 & 2)

The Kerrigan Kids
School of Potential
Myths & Magic
Kith & Kin
Playing With Power

The Queen's Alpha Series
Eternal
Everlasting
Unceasing
Evermore
Forever

Boundless
Prophecy
Protected
Foretelling
Revelation
Betrayal
Resolved

The Senseless Series
Radium Halos - Part 1
Radium Halos - Part 2
Nonsense
Perception
The Senseless - Box Set Books #1-4

Standalone
Shadow of Doubt (Part 1 & 2)
Five Shades of Fantasy
Zwarte Nevel
Shadow of Doubt - Part 1
Shadow of Doubt - Part 2
Four and a Half Shades of Fantasy
Dream Fighter
What Creeps in the Night
Forest of the Forbidden
Arcane Forest: A Fantasy Anthology
The First Fantasy Box Set

Watch for more at www.wjmaybooks.com.

Copyright 2020 by W.J. May

THIS E-BOOK OR PRINT is licensed for your personal enjoyment only. This e-book/paperback may not be re-sold or given away to other people. If you would like to share this book with another person, please purchase an additional copy for each recipient. If you're reading this book and did not purchase it, or it was not purchased for your use only, then please return to Smashwords.com and purchase your own copy. Thank you for respecting the hard work of the author.

All rights reserved. No part of this publication may be reproduced, stored in or introduced into a retrieval system, or transmitted, in any form, or by any means (electronic, mechanical, photocopying, recording, or otherwise) without the prior written permission of both the copyright owner and the above publisher of this book.

This is a work of fiction. Names, characters, places, brands, media, and incidents are either the product of the author's imagination or are used fictitiously. Any resemblance to actual person, living or dead, events, or locales is entirely coincidental. The author acknowledges the trademarked status and trademark owners of various products referenced in this work of fiction, which have been used without permission. The publication/use of these trademarks is not authorized, associated with, or sponsored by the trademark owners.

All rights reserved.
Copyright 2020 by W.J. May
Courage, Book 3 of the Omega Queen Series
Cover design by: Book Cover by Design

No part of this book may be used or reproduced in any manner whatsoever without written permission, except in the case of brief quotations embodied in articles and reviews.

Have You Read the C.o.K Series?

The Chronicles of Kerrigan
Book I - Rae of Hope is FREE!

BOOK TRAILER:
http://www.youtube.com/watch?v=gILAwXxx8MU

How hard do you have to shake the family tree to find the truth about the past?

Fifteen year-old Rae Kerrigan never really knew her family's history. Her mother and father died when she was young and it is only when she accepts a scholarship to the prestigious Guilder Boarding School in England that a mysterious family secret is revealed.

Will the sins of the father be the sins of the daughter?

As Rae struggles with new friends, a new school and a star-struck forbidden love, she must also face the ultimate challenge: receive a tattoo on her sixteenth birthday with specific powers that may bind her to an unspeakable darkness. It's up to Rae to undo the dark evil in her family's past and have a ray of hope for her future.

Find W.J. May

Website:
https://www.wjmaybooks.com
Facebook:
https://www.facebook.com/pages/Author-WJ-May-FAN-PAGE/141170442608149
Newsletter:
SIGN UP FOR W.J. May's Newsletter to find out about new releases, updates, cover reveals and even freebies!
http://eepurl.com/97aYf

Conquer Blurb:

USA Today Bestselling author, W.J. May, continues the highly anticipated bestselling YA/NA series about love, betrayal, magic and fantasy.

Be prepared to fight... it's the only option.

You wake from a dream, only to find yourself in a nightmare...

Having escaped from the sorcerer's clutches and narrowly making it across the icy plains, Evie and her friends thought the worst of their troubles were behind them. But the past has a way of catching up with you. And their problems have only begun.

Trapped in a place beyond the reach of the five kingdoms, the friends find themselves battling creatures that haven't been seen since the Dark Ages, and this time sheer luck and bravery won't be enough.

Time is running out and the Dunes are calling, but the darkness has awakened new creatures as well—dissolving past alliances and bringing chaos back to the known world.

Somewhere in the distant sand lies their salvation. Somewhere in the shadows a mysterious enemy is coming to claim it as well.

Can they get to the stone in time? Can they force a path through the danger and devastation that lies between them?

Or are some prophecies delivered too late?

BE CAREFUL WHO YOU trust. Even the devil was once an angel.

The Queen's Alpha Series

Eternal
Everlasting
Unceasing
Evermore
Forever
Boundless
Prophecy
Protected
Foretelling
Revelation
Betrayal
Resolved

The Omega Queen Series

Discipline
Bravery
Courage
Conquer
Strength
Validation
Approval
Blessing
Balance
Grievance
Enchanted
Gratified

Chapter 1

No matter how long the five friends wandered through the woods, Evie still couldn't believe that they were alive. That the pack of leopards hadn't ripped them to pieces. That the fates had seen fit to intervene. She cast a secret look at Asher, walking tall beside her. Their fingers were laced together shyly. A little smile was playing about his face. No, she couldn't believe it.

The whole thing felt like a dream.

She gave him a squeeze to make sure, blushing when he glanced down.

"You okay?" he asked softly, slowing his stride so they fell behind the others.

She nodded quickly, dropping her gaze to the ground. "My head is still spinning," she admitted. "I mean, we were given a prophecy. You learn to take some things on faith. But...*that*? One second, we're about to die? The next, we wake up here?"

The vampire stared at her a moment, then nodded.

As sunlight filtered through the trees, violent images kept flashing back through his mind. The moment when they realized they were cornered. The look on the princess' face when she stared up into his eyes. His last-second impulse to spin her around and sacrifice himself instead.

Knowing that it wouldn't actually matter. Knowing that they were both about to die.

And yet...he couldn't stop smiling?

"Well...maybe we didn't. Wake up, I mean. Maybe we did die." He gave her fingers a playful tug. "Would this be such a bad way to spend the afterlife?"

The two stared at each other for a long moment.

Then a loud voice chimed in from further up the trail.

"You are the most ghoulish people I've ever seen."

They pulled away, laughing, catching up with the others as Freya kicked pinecones petulantly down the trail. She alone didn't seem thrilled with their inexplicable rescue, mostly because she believed such a thing should never have been necessary in the first place.

"Ghoulish?" Asher echoed with a grin. "You think it's ghoulish to talk of such things? Even *now*—when we've been snatched from the jaws of death?"

"I could have gotten away on my own," she said stiffly. "If I hadn't gorged myself on elk meat right before they attacked, I would have been faster than all of you. And seeing as it was the vampire who brought us the elk...I think we all know who to blame."

Cosette and Evie burst out laughing, but Ellanden only smiled.

"No blame today. We've been blessed with a second chance. We should be endlessly grateful." He placed one foot lightly in front of the other. "No blame."

Perhaps it was that quiet gratitude, or perhaps their energy stores had simply been depleted, but the friends were moving slowly, taking their time. They'd shed the heavy winter clothes that had survived the fall from the cliff and were soaking in the sunshine, tilting their faces up to the sky.

They also didn't have a clear destination.

When they'd first awakened, Ellanden had vowed to find a landmark to get his bearings then plot the quickest course to the Dunes. Unfortunately, that landmark didn't seem to exist, and no matter how hard he tried he couldn't seem to decide upon a course.

That alone was strange.

As a people, the Fae were masters at reading the world around them. It wasn't often they'd find themselves off-balance in the middle of the woods. Ellanden didn't seem particularly troubled but, at the same time, he didn't understand. Several times, he'd glanced back at his cousin. The two of them would stare at the same thing for a moment, then she'd slowly shake her head.

"Maybe it used to be a village," she finally suggested.

The two had been having one of these silent assessments, staring at the edge of the lake. It was impossible to know what had puzzled them, but the answer didn't seem to clear things up.

"Maybe..." Ellanden murmured, but he looked unsure.

The cousins had grown up in all sorts of scenery. And while the forest around them was beautiful, it seemed to be cultivated with a bit too much care. There were intentional clusters of things. Plants that didn't usually grow together. An unnatural border to the water's edge. Lovely, to be sure. But all the loveliness in the world couldn't cover up the fact that it didn't quite make sense.

"Are you guys going to keep standing there?" Freya called sweetly. "Or can we get back to walking in circles." She held up her hands when they shot her a look. "Hey—I'm enjoying it."

"Just choose," Cosette said quietly, tuning out her friend and turning to Ellanden. "I can't see any better path than you. Just pick a direction and we can adjust on the way."

He nodded silently, glanced up at the sun, then began leading them straight west. They might not know exactly where they'd ended up, but at least they had a general direction of where they were supposed to go. And after so much uncertainty and wandering, decisive action was a welcome relief.

The friends continued with a renewed spring in their step. Confident that they'd soon come across a road or a village. Confident that the troubles that chased them were in the past.

Then they came to a sudden stop.

"What...the hell is that?"

Of all the little oddities they'd come across since waking in the forest, this one was truly impossible to ignore. A row of towering redwoods planted closely together, with their branches torn off at the sides. The friends stopped in their tracks, staring up in wonder.

"What could have done that?" Cosette murmured, taking a step closer. "Look at the roots."

Evie followed her gaze, but didn't understand what she was seeing. The trunks of the trees were normal enough, but it looked as though the bottoms had been shorn off. They were resting lightly upon the ground instead of growing up from within it.

She spun around as she tried to see what was holding them up, what was holding them all together. Then there was a sudden *crash* and the five of them froze.

No one dared to speak. No one dared to move. They'd been through enough trauma in the last few days not to draw attention to themselves now.

But those crashes were getting louder...heading straight for them.

We should have run.

By the time the thought occurred to them, it was already too late. The row of trees swung open and the baffling figure of a man swept inside. He was dragging the carcass of one of the leopards behind him, tossing it in the middle of the grass. The princess suddenly understood why the creatures stayed mainly on the ice plain, why large chunks had been torn out of their skin.

Then the trees swung shut behind him.

She blinked, in a kind of daze.

Swung open. Swung shut.

Her heart froze in her chest.

It's a gate...

The friends lifted their heads slowly.

...and that's a giant.

Pure. Absolute. Panic.

"Run!"

She wasn't sure who'd whispered, but they all started moving at the same time—staying close together, keeping to the underbrush as much as possible. It was clear they'd been brought for a reason, it was clear what had 'saved' them in the woods. Not some kindly fate after all, but a savage creature capable of delivering an even more terrifying death.

There was no way to fight such a thing, and there was no way to run. The only thing they had going for them was that giants were notoriously distractible, and at the moment dismembering the leopard seemed more important than wondering where he'd placed his little trophies.

Their only chance was to get away before he found out.

In a sudden burst of speed, the five friends bolted across the open grass to the gate. But just seconds before they got there, it swung open again of its own accord. That could have ended things right there. As the redwoods went flying towards them, they dove backwards before they could get crushed by the impact. The second they landed the five of them scrambled into the underbrush, holding on to each other as the ground trembled and a whole troop of other giants arrived on the scene. The gate swung shut behind them, knocking the teenagers right off their feet.

Seven hells...there's a whole clan!

There wasn't much known about the history of giants. Mostly because if someone was unfortunate enough to encounter one, they usually didn't survive to tell the tale. There were a few outliers, a few that had shunned the bloodthirsty reputation and retreated to live on their own. But for the most part, the consensus was the same. In terms of supernatural creatures, giants were about as savage as you could get. They delighted in violence, reveled in destruction, and could rip apart just about anything you could think of with those massive, brutish hands.

In a lot of ways, they were like vampires. Only much, *much* bigger.

And the clan in question was certainly living up to their name.

"Where is it?!"

The friends shrank back into the grass as the tallest of the bunch stomped forward, shaking the ground with every step of its enormous feet. He had a shock of grizzled black hair and the same dark beady eyes as the rest of them. Eyes that locked on the dead leopard with instant greed.

"My kill! My cat!"

They stared at him in astonishment, then glanced quickly at the carcass. It was still lying in pieces behind the one who'd dragged it inside, leaking brackish blood all over the ground.

Evie's stomach twisted in preemptive knots at the prospect of him eating such a thing, but no sooner had he stepped forward than he was shoved all the way back to the gate.

"MY kill! MY cat!"

Their heads spun around to the first giant, the one who'd almost squashed them when he'd first arrived. He might not have been quite as tall as the other, but he was bigger—so big that he was bursting straight out of the worn leather sleeves stretched around his arms.

There was something territorial about the way he was standing, not just with the leopard but with everything past the gate. The princess wondered suddenly if this patch of earth was the place he'd decided to call home. It would explain the gate, the intentional design of the flora. It wasn't a forest at all—the friends had been wandering around the giant's garden.

There was a strange rumbling sound and her eyes flashed back to the imposter. He was still looking at the dead cat jealously, his fingers curling into meaty fists. It took her a second to realize the deafening rumbling was actually coming from his stomach. Her knees curled back to her chest.

"...share?"

The friends' eyebrows shot up at the same time, astonished that such a word was in a giant's vocabulary. There was a charged moment where nothing happened, then the first giant yanked off one of the leopard's legs and tossed it through the air. It flipped twice, spraying the garden with blood, before the second giant caught it with a surprisingly agile hand. His eyes gleamed with anticipation before he tore off the mottled fur and ripped into it with his teeth.

It was quite possibly the most horrific thing the princess had ever seen. The girls covered their eyes. The Prince of the Fae flinched. Even the vampire, bred with his own kind of savagery, took a single look before twisting his head away, looking as though he might be sick.

The leopard had been huge—the size of a small house. But the giants made quick work of it, inhaling the meat until there was nothing left but splintered bones which they tossed back and forth at each other, roaring with laughter as each struck with enough force to shatter stone.

And when they finish with those? What comes next?

Evie glanced at the others—pale and frozen—watching the spectacle with such terrified attention they were unable to tear their eyes away. Two times she had to pull on Ellanden's sleeve before he finally broke his gaze, looking down at her in silent panic.

"We need to leave."

It was so obvious, yet it hadn't occurred to any of them. After that initial burst of flight their bodies had instinctually locked down, overwhelmed with the paralyzing instinct to hide.

Ellanden glanced once more at the giants, then forced himself to nod.

As quietly as possible they grabbed the others, dragging them to cover behind the nearest tree. From there, they could hear the monsters but not see them. It made it easier to breathe.

"All right," the fae whispered, "simple plan. Just stay down, and stay quiet. The gate's less than twenty paces away and they're distracted. With any luck, they'll never remember we were—"

The tree was ripped out of the ground.

"—here."

There was a split second where nothing happened. The giants stared at the gang, and the gang stared at the giants. Then one of them spat out a piece of bone, and all hell broke loose.

With a wild shout, the friends scattered in opposite directions. The fae sprinted straight into the trees, the witch shrouded herself in fog and slipped towards the gate. The vampire grabbed the princess in his arms, ghosting through the woods like smoke.

Except...none of that mattered.

A filthy hand reached down from the sky, knocking Asher off his feet and wrapping around the princess' waist. She let out an involuntary scream as she was yanked into the air. Then the hand tightened and she sucked in a gasping breath, staring in stunned silence at the creature holding her.

The others had no better luck.

Before Asher could get to his feet the giant who'd demanded the carcass stepped on his cloak, tripping him once more before grabbing him by the back of the neck. Another disappeared into the underbrush, emerging a moment later with Ellanden and Cosette in each hand. The one who'd caught Freya was absolutely delighted when she fired back with a spray of neon sparks. He let out a roar of laughter, demanding that she do it again, shaking her upside-down so quickly he didn't seem to realize she'd already blacked out. When Ellanden tried a similar maneuver, burying a sword in his captor's hand, the giant holding him glanced down in surprise, then flicked it away like it was nothing more than a splinter, inadvertently slashing the prince at the same time.

It was in that moment Evie realized a terrifying truth: they could be killed just as easily by accident as by some intentional design. Tempers were rising, adrenaline was flowing, and the more her friends struggled the more likely it was. Under no circumstances could she allow that to happen.

"STOP!" she screamed at the top of her lungs.

Eight pairs of eyes shot towards her—some giants, some friends. It was hard to say who looked more surprised. To be honest, it was hard to tell how much the giants could register at all.

"What is it—" She braced herself against the suffocating grip around her ribcage, trying to shift herself higher to find the air to breathe. "What is it you want from us?"

At this point, the question was a bit superfluous. They'd been caught by a pack of bloodthirsty savages—did it really matter as to the reason why? But simply saying the words out loud stopped the dangerous build of momentum. For a moment, everyone in the garden was still.

The giant holding her looked down curiously, tilting his head a bit to the side.

"Red hair...like fire."

Not too much like fire. Please—oh, please—don't get it into your head to set us on fire.

The princess tilted her entire body towards him, trying hard to meet his gaze. It was difficult, considering the vise-like grip of his fingers, but she didn't see any menace in his face. There was nothing but honest curiosity, along with an inexplicable bit of pride.

Again—she asked the question.

"What do you want?"

This time, she was genuinely interested in the answer. All of them combined wouldn't make a single meal for even one of the giants. They couldn't have been brought only for that purpose. At any rate, they wouldn't have been left unattended in the garden. The gate might have been tall, but it was slatted. There were places where the friends could slip through.

The giant continued to stare at her in open fascination before lifting his eyes with a smile.

"Mine."

The entire garden fell silent.

Evie shook her head once, then went rigid—not quite understanding, but vaguely aware it was the worst thing he could have said. Before she could come up with a response, he spoke again.

"All four—*mine*."

Four?

As if on cue, the shifty-looking giant who'd demanded a share of the cat made to slip Asher casually into his pocket. If the vampire hadn't started screaming, he might have gotten away with it.

"Five!" Asher cried, waving his arms frantically. "There are five of us!"

The giant holding Evie looked over with a frown, then stormed towards them—striking the other across the face before holding out his open palm. "They are MINE!"

There was a terrifying pause, then the vampire was passed between them—handed off like he was some kind of toy. The princess watched with wide eyes, then suddenly she understood.

"A pet?" she asked in terror. "You...you want a pet?"

The giant reached out a stubby finger, stroking Asher's dark hair, concussing him in the process. His eyes gleamed possessively, gesturing for the others to relinquish their trophies as well.

"Now I have four."

There was a beat of silence.

"Five," Freya couldn't help but correct. The others looked at her incredulously and she grimaced with a shrug. "Sorry, it's just...there are five."

Evie stared up at the giant in horror. There was no way he was serious. It had to be a joke.

But there was no deception in those beady eyes. Giants didn't do deception. When you had that much brute strength, word games were a bit superfluous.

The monster was lonely. And the others wouldn't dare challenge him.

It was as simple as that.

"Go home," he commanded, pointing at the gate. "Leave now."

A rather abrupt dismissal, but social niceties didn't seem to be high on a giant's list of priorities. Instead he reached out greedily as the rest of his clan left, collecting the friends one by one. They tumbled free of the fingers that held them, spilling awkwardly onto his open palm.

The fae were too disoriented to stage any kind of escape, and Freya rolled out of her captor's hand so violently she almost fell off the other side. The giant caught her at the last moment, holding them all smashed up together as if proud that he'd collected the entire set.

"Mine."

The gate swung shut in the distance, adding a ringing finality to the words.

A heavy silence descended upon them.

Evie and Asher were staring in shocked silence. Cosette and Freya were being crushed so tight they couldn't breathe. Ellanden was keeping his jaws clenched together, like if he didn't there was a good chance he might scream. Then the giant smiled again and gestured over his shoulder.

"Home."

Only then did they notice what had been previously kept out of sight. The entrance was mostly hidden behind a cluster of cedars, but held at such an elevation it was suddenly easy to see the basic framework of a cottage. Four simple walls, a chimney, and a massive air-tight door.

Without another word, the giant began carrying them inside.

That's when the screaming began for real.

There was simply no stopping it. It was physically impossible to keep quiet when something ten times your size was dragging you away. The friends fought uselessly against his fingers. Cosette managed to catch hold of the door frame, her fingernails leaving long grooves in the wood.

A second later, the door shut behind them.

The screaming stopped. There was no point to it anymore. There was no getting out.

Chapter 2

From one cage to another.

Evie leaned back against the bars, staring blankly out the window. It was mounted so high she never would have been able to see it otherwise, but as fate would have it they were dangling pretty high themselves. When the giant had pushed through the cottage door, it became clear that the five friends weren't his first attempt at kidnapping some company—though they might have been the first people. He'd taken one look around, then walked straight to the center of the room and thrust them into a rounded, oversized bird cage hanging from the ceiling on a chain.

Where he'd gotten such a massive item was a complete mystery. As was the prehistoric bird that was clearly meant to go inside. At this point, the friends could only hope it was gone for good as they sat in the metal circle, legs stretched out in front of them, resting their heads against the bars.

"I can't believe this," Ellanden muttered, glaring a hole into the floor.

It wasn't the first time he'd said it, nor would it be the last. But by now, the others were too exhausted to engage him. It felt like years ago that they'd woken up on that icy plain. The leopard attack seemed like another lifetime. As did their walk through the forest, their fall off the icy cliff.

"...*cannot* believe it..."

Evie turned with a sigh to Cosette. "How's your head?"

The young fae had struck it violently against the ceiling of the cage when they were thrust inside. Just a tad more force, and there was a decent chance she wouldn't have opened her eyes.

"It's fine," she murmured, lifting a hand just to be sure. A delicate wince rippled across her face, but she refused to acknowledge it. "Just fine."

"You know," Freya began testily, "now would have been a *great* time to pull out that handy seeing stone. We could have dropped it into the water dish. Your dad would be on the way."

Evie shot her a look of warning, while Cosette glared through a tangle of blood-matted hair. "I said I was sorry for the stone."

The witch smiled sweetly. "And now we're *all* sorry for it."

"...can't believe it..."

"Would you stop?" Evie snapped, shooting a glare at Ellanden. "We get it, okay?"

He glared back just as fiercely. "I'm sorry if I'm having a little trouble wrapping my head around this," he replied with bitter sarcasm. "It's just that we're sitting in an enormous birdcage because some relic from the Stone Age decided he wanted a *pet*! What the hell does that mean anyway? We're the size of his thumb! What interest could the creature possibly have?"

"It isn't that strange," Asher said grimly. "Imagine if your childhood toys suddenly came to life. Wouldn't you want them to play?"

"This is *not* the same thing," Ellanden answered stiffly.

"Oh, would you guys drop it already?" Freya interrupted, shifting uncomfortably before closing her eyes. "This is bad enough without all the squabbling."

Cosette stared at her for a long moment. "There's a human ribcage behind your head."

The witch glanced over her shoulder, then let out a shriek and bolted forward, sending the bones crashing to the floor. They shattered upon impact, scattering to different corners of the room.

Five heads appeared above them, staring down from the cage.

"Well I guess that answers the question of whether or not we can get out," Evie muttered.

"Maybe not," Ellanden countered hopefully, his dark eyes sweeping over the room. "If I could force through the bars and make it to that window—"

"And then what?" Asher finally lost his temper, glaring across the cage. "You'd break through the glass? There's *no way* out, Ellanden."

"Well at least I'm trying—"

The cage fell silent as the door swung open and the giant came back inside. He stretched up his massive arms before striding to the center of the room, giving the cage a playful shake.

A 'playful shake' that sent the friends crashing into the bars.

"Fall down," he chortled, shaking it again. "Funny."

He thinks this is FUNNY?!

Evie slid back to the base of the cage, discreetly grabbing the bars behind her, glaring up at the giant with all her might. The others took the same defensive position but Ellanden pushed to his feet and stood straight in the middle of the circle, as if challenging the giant to get a closer look.

The giant was more than happy to oblige.

With a look of almost childlike excitement, he flipped up the metal latch and opened the door to the cage. A greedy hand reached inside, fingers grasping and ready. But the second the door was open, Ellanden vaulted off the creature's wrist and made a running leap for freedom.

There were few things in the world faster than a fae. A vampire was one. A grimlock was another. Before that day, Evie wouldn't have thought to add 'giant' to that list.

But she would have been wrong.

In a flash, his hand shot out again—snatching Ellanden straight out of the air. The fae let out a painful gasp as he was jerked backwards, then struggled automatically as those fingers wrapped around his ribs. He gave up a moment later, realizing it was useless. When the giant thrust him back into the cage, he held perfectly still—watching as the creature leaned closer to look him in the eyes.

"One mouth."

The others were still staring in confusion when he jabbed a finger inside the cage, prodding at the fae. Ellanden sucked in a quick breath and twisted his head. It looked as though his jaw was broken, but when the giant waited for confirmation, he somehow managed to speak.

"One mouth."

The giant nodded with satisfaction, then tilted his head.

"One chest."

Before the fae could react he flicked him in the center of the ribs, knocking him to the floor with such force it was all he could do not to cry out in pain. The cage rattled and he rolled onto his side a moment later, a bracing arm wrapped around his torso.

"One...one chest."

The giant's eyes glittered in the darkness, watching as he pushed shakily to his feet. There was a moment where he said nothing. Then he leaned ever so slightly closer.

"One hand."

The fae looked up at him slowly.

"...*two* hands."

The giant stared back, intent.

"One hand."

A charged silence fell over the room. The fae slowly backed into the cage.

The door slammed shut a moment later and the giant swept out of sight. Just three large steps and he was already back outside, whistling under his breath as he went off to find some other unholy carcass to eat for dinner. Ellanden stared after him for a long time, then turned to the rest.

"I vote we stay here forever."

It wasn't funny. It *really* wasn't funny.

But whether it was a delayed-shock reaction or simply the fact that they were dangling fifty feet off the ground in a bird cage, Evie found herself trying not to laugh.

"Forever, huh? The guy convinced you?"

Ellanden nodded swiftly, not seeming to notice the way he kept gripping his wrists. Eternally grateful they were still attached to the rest of his body.

"Furthermore, I'll turn you in if you try to escape," he continued. "Shriek for help, jump and point—all that."

This time, the laughter wasn't hers alone. The bickering stopped and the tension between them vanished as Asher swiftly got to his feet, helping his shell-shocked friend to the floor.

"That's very gallant of you," he answered with an amused smile, gently tilting the fae's head back and forth to survey the damage. "Particularly the shrieking."

Ellanden nodded stiffly, staring at the ceiling while the vampire examined his jaw. "Yes, well...I'm known for being gallant."

Asher pulled back with a sympathetic smile. "I think he broke your mouth."

"Yep. Feels that way."

THE NEXT DAY, WHEN the giant came back, the friends tried a different ploy.

While the rest of them remained around the edges, leaning back against the bars, the princess was sprawled in the middle of the circle. Face-down. Crimson hair splayed over the floor.

The giant took a single look, then his eyes tightened in concern.

"Asleep?"

Asher shook his head slowly, pure murder in his eyes. "She's not asleep. She's *dead*. You killed her last night."

It wasn't a stretch of the imagination. Sometime in the early hours of the morning, the giant had gone outside to relieve himself. On the way back in, he'd stumbled in the darkness and smacked his head into the cage. A bruise for him, several hairline fractures for his new pets. Evie had gotten some of the worst of it—being thrown straight into the ceiling before crashing down to the floor.

Coincidentally, that's when the friends got the idea to stage another escape.

"Dead?" the giant repeated in surprise.

Evie lay very still, eyes closed, trying to breathe as little as possible. She felt the cage sway as the creature leaned forward for a better look. She suddenly wondered if he had a name.

"Yes—dead," Asher snapped, hoping very much the giant would take their word for it. At worst, she'd be left in the trashcan. At best, he'd put her outside. Either way, she'd get past the bars of the cage. "What did you expect? You can't be so rough."

The giant stared another moment, then lifted his shoulders sadly. "Food, then."

WAIT, WHAT?!

"Hang on—I was wrong!" Asher cried as she scrambled to her feet, retreating hastily to blend in with the others. "See? It looks like she got better!"

The giant leaned closer, blinking slowly.

"Better?" When the princess gave an awkward wave, his mouth fell open in a gap-toothed smile. "All better! Nothing can stay dead for long."

He reached out happily, but Cosette caught the back of her shirt—yanking her discreetly out of sight. There was a moment of confusion then he leaned down to examine all of them, resting his chin against the base of the cage as he greedily surveyed his prizes.

"Pointy teeth?"

Evie glanced at Asher, half-surprised the giant had recognized what he was. Scurrying about so far below them she'd assumed that, to giants, people of the kingdoms all looked the same.

The vampire took a step back, making a conscious effort not to bare his fangs.

He'd seen what had happened to Ellanden. A careless flick of his finger and those teeth could get knocked out for good. Fortunately, the giant had the attention span of an under-motivated goldfish. His beady eyes locked on Asher for only a moment before roving delightedly over the flowers sewn into the hem of Freya's dress.

"Pretty!"

He gave them a tug and the entire dress came off her shoulders, caught only by Ellanden's quick hands. She let out a yelp, leaning back with the fabric gathered around her chest, then shamelessly hid behind the fae when the giant reached for her again.

"Careful," Ellanden tempered, holding up his hands. He thought better of it a moment later, and hid them both behind his back. "You need to be careful, remember?"

It seemed a foolish strategy, speaking to the giant as if he was a child, but it seemed to have the desired effect. The giant lowered his hand, staring at the fae with a puzzled expression.

"White?"

The prince lifted his eyebrows and glanced at the others. But they didn't seem to have any better idea than he did himself. Then Evie cupped a hand over her mouth.

"Your hair," she whispered. "He's talking about your hair."

Ellanden lifted his eyes, hoping the giant wouldn't want a closer look. "Oh...yeah, it's white."

The giant was puzzled. Ellanden didn't look old, but he had no other explanation for such a thing. Then his eyes drifted to Cosette's ivory locks and he drew the only possible conclusion.

"Married."

The fae glanced at each other before Ellanden quickly shook his head.

"No, not married. We're actually—"

"*Married*," the giant said firmly, gesturing between them. Not only was he pleased to have solved the mystery, but he was slightly proud—as if he'd only just learned the word.

The fae nodded quickly.

"Okay—married."

The giant settled back down, looking satisfied. Twice, his eyes circled the cage. Each time, they came to rest on the princess. He sighed contentedly, staring with a lazy smile.

"Happy not dead. My favorite."

She tried to smile back, then cast a terrified look at the others.

...jealous?

The giant stared a moment longer, then abruptly grabbed her out of the cage. "You come with me now."

Evie let out a gasp, stunned by the speed of it, but there was nothing she could do. Those fingers had curled around her once again, and no sooner had she registered their presence than she was being lifted out of the cage and carried across the floor.

"NO!" Asher shouted, lunging after them.

Ellanden quickly caught him by the cloak, yanking him back before the giant could notice, but the vampire was beside himself. Instead of trying to pull away he smashed his head backwards, deliberately hitting the prince in the mouth. Ellanden let out a soft cry, releasing him while torrents of blood poured down his chin, but Freya stopped him as well. A vampire versus a witch. A slender hand rose to his chest. But the tips of her fingers were glowing.

"You'll get yourself killed," she murmured, serious as Evie had ever heard. "Chances are you'll get her killed as well. *Breathe*, Ash. He's not going to hurt her."

Whatever Asher said in reply, the princess would never hear it. They may have been trapped inside a simple cabin, but it was a cabin with giant-sized dimensions. By the time they reached the opposite side of the room she could barely make out her friends, still dangling in their little prison.

Without the slightest hope of a rescue, she turned her attention back to the giant.

He was whistling again, creaking the floorboards as he threw another piece of wood onto the roaring fire. The princess let out a shriek when the flames climbed higher—scrambling uselessly against the back of his hand. But he simply chuckled and sank down into a crudely-made rocking chair, reaching back behind him onto a shelf. A moment later, he dropped a book onto his lap. A book approximately the size of the royal equestrian ring back at the castle.

Evie's hair flew back as she stared up at him with wide eyes.

"Read."

Where would a giant get a book? It would have to be from another giant. It isn't like they sell these things at the village library. I wonder how—

"Read!"

Her hair flew back again as he repeated the demand, jabbing at the dusty cover with his finger. She glanced between them without the slightest idea how to get such a thing done.

"I don't..." she trailed off uncertainly. "Is it in the common tongue—"

Instead of answering, he flipped open the cover and plopped her down at the top of the very first page. Each letter was the size of her head. She had to stand on the tips of toes if she wanted to get enough distance to see the entire word. But giant was waiting. And giants didn't wait long.

"Back when the world was young, when dragons ruled the skies and kraken ruled the seas, Arsinia the Cruel set out on her maiden voyage..."

Evie's eyes flashed up, but the giant was reclining—rocking back and forth with a bizarrely peaceful expression on his face. She cast another helpless look towards the cage, wondering if there was a way to renounce her title as favorite, before he cleared his throat and she yelped.

"The seas were rough, churning with winter storms, but Arsinia had no fear..."

It was a simple story, in a layout impossible for someone of regular size. In order to keep pace, the princess found herself running back and forth—completing one arduous line, only to race back across the page to begin the next. The heat of the fire was making her dizzy. By the time she finished the first two pages, she was panting for breath.

Why does he want me to do this? Why does a giant even have a book?

As if reading her thoughts, the giant shifted contentedly. One hand kept the book steady, while the other lifted her gently and flipped the page.

"Good book." His eyes peeked open for a split second. "My mother."

Even amidst the bizarre situation, Evie's mouth fell open in surprise.

"Arsinia?" she asked. "Arsinia is your mother?"

Arsinia the *Cruel*—her mind tagged on quickly. But it gave way to other things. 'Back when the world was young, when dragons ruled the skies and kraken ruled the seas.'

She stared up at him hesitantly. "How long do giants live?"

His eyes closed again as the rocking began anew. "Long time. Sometimes...too long."

She considered this a moment, staring down at the next line of writing scribbled across the page. After a few seconds, her eyes flickered up to the cage.

"It must get lonely," she murmured.

The giant prodded the book once again, making her fall right off her feet.

"Read," he commanded, closing his eyes once more.

She pushed slowly to her feet, shoved curtains of hair from her face, then began the little workout all over again—racing back and forth across the page.

She couldn't even imagine how it must have looked from a distance. She couldn't even imagine what her parents would say if they could see her now. Scrambling back and forth across a boat-sized copy of *Arsinia the Cruel*. A giant snoring in the rocking chair just below.

She'd met a giant only one time before—her mother's friend, Bernie. While her father had been incredibly hesitant to let her go her mother had led the way down to his cottage, rambling on and on about how they were expected for lunch and couldn't be late.

Her parents had all sorts of weird things like that. A company of dwarves that somehow made their way past the Belarian Royal Guard just to surprise her father in his chambers. A trio of fairies that dropped out of the sky whenever there was mention of free food. She'd long ago learned not to question it and simply roll with the punches...but this? They would have some pretty strong feelings about this. Just to start—

Wait...snoring?

The princess paused her story, glancing slowly over her shoulder only to see the giant in question passed out in his chair. His mouth was hanging open and little trickles of drool were streaming down his chin. If there was ever a chance to escape...

In a flash, she leapt off the book—sliding down the length of the chair until her feet hit the floor. Once there, she peered back up at the giant. He hadn't moved an inch.

Okay...just think.

While she might be free to roam about the floor her friends were still trapped up in that cage, and she had no way to reach them. Even if she could somehow get them down, the door was shut and they didn't have the slightest chance of opening it.

Ellanden's right...our best shot is the window.

Armed with that small flicker of hope, she took off running once more. Hoping that Freya could use some handy spell to coax open the glass. Hoping that she could reach the birdcage before their nameless giant woke up in a huff, wondering what happened to Arsinia's magic axe.

"Please see me," she whispered as she streaked across the floor and neared the bottom of the cage. "Please be looking..."

Sure enough, four heads appeared instantly above her—staring down with equal parts relief and shock. They vanished for a split second, probably having some kind of conference, then reappeared a second later. At the same time, they started pointing wildly to the corner of the room.

The princess followed their gaze to a mop propped up in the corner. *The smoke is getting to them. They've been up there too long.*

Even so far away, she could see Ellanden roll his eyes. With exaggerated slowness, he mimed knocking the mop over—angling it so the handle fell against the bars of the cage. At that point the friends would assumedly break through the bars, slide down the handle, and make it out the window before the giant had a chance to open his eyes.

...not the greatest plan.

...but it was all they had.

Evie took a deep breath and nodded, changing direction mid-course and sprinting over to the mop. She had no idea how she'd knock the thing over, any more than she knew why a giant would have a mop in the first place. The handle was longer than most trees. It wasn't like she could just give the base of it a shove—

All at once she froze, cocking her head as she listened to the world around her. Something was different. She couldn't tell exactly what it was, but something wasn't right. Then it hit her.

The room was quiet. The snoring had stopped.

No sooner had her friends started screaming than a hand flew out of nowhere and she was yanked straight off her feet. The world vanished in a rush of wind and crimson hair, and her hands clamped over her mouth in a vain attempt to silence her own scream. Her body tried to curl into a defensive position, but she was stopped by the thick fingers wrapped around her waist. When she finally lifted her head, she found herself staring into a pair of enormous beady eyes.

"Silly girl...nowhere to run."

Her teeth sank into her lower lip as tears spilled freely down her face. She could hear her friends shouting above her. She was just inches from the monster's mouth.

Then all at once, that mouth curved in a lopsided smile.

"The story's not finished."

Chapter 3

By the time Evie finished recounting the tales of Arsinia the Cruel, the sun was just beginning to come up over the horizon. The giant had fallen asleep for the most of it, but after her escape attempt had been thwarted she didn't dare stop. Every time she considered she needed only to think of those massive, mossy teeth before continuing with a renewed sense of urgency.

But the book was finally finished. And the princess was dead on her feet.

It was a testament to her state of mind, that when the giant lifted her from the pages and carried her back to the cage she hardly noticed. Nor did she notice when he dumped her inside, and shortly after picked up a bucket by the front door. It wasn't until a torrent of icy water splashed through the bars, soaking her head to toe, that she blinked slowly, vowing to kill herself before the end of the day.

"Rise and shine," the giant called cheerfully, watching as the others leapt to their feet with a gasp, spitting out mouthfuls of icy sludge. "Something to drink!"

On that charming note, he headed back into the forest—whistling as he went.

The gang stood in silence as water streamed off of them, plastering their hair and clothes to their bodies before pouring out the bottom of the cage. Their first instinct was to start protesting, but that wouldn't do any good. Their next instinct was to complain, but that wouldn't do any good either. In the end they merely sat back down, shivering and glaring all the while.

"Welcome back!"

Unlike the others, whose moods had plummeted, Freya seemed determined to be in good spirits—quite possibly because she was the only one who'd dodged the bulk of the flood. With an inexplicably bright smile, she bounded up to the recently-returned princess—leaning in for a hug before rethinking it and giving her a wet pat on the shoulder instead.

"That was quite the workout, huh? Who knew that reading a book could double as cardio?" She faltered at the look on Evie's face. "I'm just saying, it could be worse."

The princess slowly lifted her eyebrows, dripping head to toe. "You mean because he didn't *eat* me?"

The witch nodded soundly, flashing a bright smile. "Exactly! He hasn't eaten a single one of us!"

Our standards have gotten depressingly low.

"No," Ellanden muttered caustically, "he just wants us to read him stories and get married."

"Come on," Asher said darkly, "it'd be cute. He could march you down the aisle like dolls."

Usually one to find the humor, the fae didn't crack a smile.

"That's right, because if there's one thing that could make this situation better it's being forced to marry my cousin in some bloody forsaken cage."

Freya bit her lip sympathetically. "Hey, it could be…"

The fae shot her a look and she adjusted mid-sentence.

"Nope. That's pretty much as bad as it gets."

Evie glanced between them then shuffled to the opposite side of the circle, sinking to the wet metal and bringing her knees up to her chest. Asher was beside her a moment later, sitting close but not too close, giving her space while trying to be supportive at the same time.

He watched her carefully from the corner of his eye, just as he'd been watching throughout the entire night. She took a second to collect herself, to reconcile with the shock of what she'd just spent the last few hours doing. Then her eyes tightened as silent tears began pouring down her face.

She was in his arms a second later, sobbing quietly into his chest. "I can't believe...I can't believe that just happened."

The vampire closed his eyes, pressing a soft kiss to the top of her head. "I know."

The others paused their caustic banter, feeling guilty to have started it in the first place. Once it had become clear that the giant had no intention of actually harming the princess, they'd let basic survival instinct take over and compartmentalized what they were seeing to process on a later day.

Asher had been unable to do that, living and dying with each breath.

"Can I get you something to drink?" he asked softly.

She lifted her head with a shaky laugh. "Whiskey?"

He nodded thoughtfully, pretending to consider. "How about...water from the bottom of a bird cage?"

She laughed again, still holding fistfuls of his shirt. "Ash, I just..." A wave of panic took hold and she forgot what she'd been saying, changing direction mid-course. "How are we going to get out of here?"

His lips parted automatically, then closed—thinning to a hard line as he stared helplessly across the room. Helpless wasn't an emotion vampires were familiar with. Neither was desperation.

And yet, looking into those crying eyes, he suddenly felt both.

"I don't know," he said softly, tightening the circle of his arms. Her heart was racing, pulsing through them both, and a sudden sense of determination burned through him. He leaned back a moment later, staring deep into her eyes. "But I *swear* to you, Evie...I'm going to get us out."

Still buzzing with that surge of adrenaline, still tingling with a heartbeat that wasn't his own, he gave her a final squeeze. Then pushed slowly to his feet, eyes flying around the length of the cabin.

Unlike the others, his eyes were designed for greater distances. The only ones who came close were the fae, but after Ellanden's initial escape had almost resulted in dismemberment he'd put all further plans temporarily on hold. Asher had no such qualms.

One way or another, they were getting out of this cage.

Little things jumped out at him. Things the others wouldn't think twice about, but a lifetime of getting out of scrapes with his father brought them to the forefront of his mind.

The giant couldn't see well in the dark: he'd left a lantern on the table.

The giant couldn't breathe well in smoke: he'd cracked the window when he started a fire.

The final piece of the puzzle clicked into place when the giant himself came back into the cabin, throwing a handful of roots down onto the table. He was hungry. So were they.

"Making some lunch?" he called down loudly, wrapping his hands around the bars of the cage. The others glanced up in alarm, while the giant's hands paused curiously over the roots. "Must be nice. We'd love some food, too. It's been days and you've kept us here with nothing to eat."

Ironic words, coming from a vampire. It was fairly certain he couldn't eat anything the giant might give him. But the giant didn't consider this. And Asher had other things on his mind.

"What are you doing?" Evie hissed, afraid to make herself seen, on the off-chance that Arsinia the Cruel had a sequel. "You really want him to throw us some rotting leopard meat?"

The vampire ignored her, turning to Ellanden instead. "Go with me on this."

The fae stared back with wide eyes, but nodded—quickly pushing to his feet. With great hesitation he joined his friend at the wall of the cage, staring at the giant.

"Ellanden said you wouldn't know what to feed us," Asher continued authoritatively. "He thinks that's probably why you've never been able to keep other pets."

The fae shot him a quick look of betrayal, then turned bracingly to the giant.

"It's true," he called, grimacing. "There obviously used to be a bird in here, but I'm pretty sure it's dead. Did you forget to feed that as well?"

A spark of anger flashed through the giant's eyes as he leaned threateningly across the kitchen table, wielding the large knife he was using for the roots.

"Didn't forget *anything*," he snarled. "Bird choked on smaller bird."

The men fell momentarily silent, not knowing what to make of this. Then Asher sighed loudly and leaned against the walls of the cage, pretending he didn't really care either way.

"Sounds pretty irresponsible to me," he said off-handedly. "But then, I'm not the one with his reputation on the line. You're the one who'd have to explain it to all your friends."

The giant stomped his foot in frustration, sending a shockwave through the walls. The cage rattled and the lantern on the table tipped precariously before righting itself. Asher shot a fleeting glance at Ellanden, who nodded as a look of understanding lit his eyes.

"I don't understand why we ended up here anyway," the fae continued, glancing around the cage as if the entire thing was rather beneath him. "The one who caught you was much taller."

"That's true..." Asher said thoughtfully, frowning as he remembered. "Probably stronger, too. I wonder if it's too late to suggest a trade."

At this point, the giant was beside himself. In one fell swoop he crossed the length of the cabin, that enormous blade flailing wildly in his hands.

"NOT taller! NOT stronger!"

Ellanden kept a watchful eye on the knife, but answered with a shrug. "Looked that way to me. He could probably tear right through the bars of this—"

A streak of silver flashed towards them.

"—cage."

With a scream of frustration, the giant swung the knife straight at their dangling prison. It lodged in the metal with a reverberating *gong* that rattled the friends to the core, starting in their boots and ending in their teeth. None of them was able to stay standing. The only reason the boys kept their heads was because the knife didn't happen to make it all the way through.

But it was close enough. So close that, when the giant pried it free again, the metal bars tore through with a defeated screech, leaving a thin sliver of sunlight leaking between the pieces.

A stunned silence followed the outburst. One that left the gang so shaken, Ellanden didn't even see it coming when the giant stuck his fingers through the cage and grabbed him by the shirt.

"THERE!" he shouted directly at the stricken prince. "STRONG ENOUGH FOR YOU?"

The fae froze where he stood, white as a sheet. When he lifted a hand to his ear, it came away bleeding. He stared in shock, then hid it quickly—giants were notoriously excited by the sight of blood. But for the moment, their giant had far greater issues on his mind.

The rampage was only just beginning.

With another wounded howl he kicked through his bookshelves, punched a hole in the rocking chair. In a matter of seconds he worked his way through the entire cabin, leaving a trail of wreckage in his wake. When he finally returned to the kitchen he smashed his fists into the center of the table, breaking one of the legs and shattering the lantern at the same time. A wave of kerosene rushed across the wood, soaking the roots he was preparing to cook.

Of course, this made him scream even louder.

"STUPID PETS!" he thundered. "NOW I HAVE TO START ALL OVER!"

Without another word, he stormed out of the house—slamming the door as he stomped right through the center of his beloved garden. The friends flinched at the sound. All except the prince, who was still staring after him in a state of shock.

"Landi," Asher called quickly, rushing over to him.

The fae glanced up in surprise at the hands clamped down on his shoulders. It was only then that Evie realized he couldn't hear them. The giant's shouting had made him temporarily deaf.

He turned a bit unsteadily, staring at the vampire before hitting him right in the face. "Great plan."

Asher bowed his head with a grin, wiping away a streak of blood. "It was a great start," he murmured, though only the girls could hear him. "The rest is yet to come..."

THE SUN HAD FALLEN, and still the giant had yet to return to the cabin. Given the state of how he left, there was a good chance he was off arm-wrestling every other giant in the five kingdoms. But it quickly became clear that whatever Asher was planning couldn't happen until he came back.

He could, however, do a little prep-work.

"Can you help me with this?" he called across the cage.

The rest of the friends were sprawled listlessly over the floor. Three days without a bite to eat were starting to wear on each of them; particularly the princess, who'd spent the entire night running back and forth across the same wretched book. They'd put up with the vampire's antics as best they could, especially considering the first part of his plan had almost resulted in a group decapitation. When he was unwilling to tell them the second part, on the grounds they wouldn't dare attempt such a thing, they'd disowned him completely, preferring to starve in petulant silence.

"Anybody?" he insisted, rattling the bars of the cage. "Anybody at all?"

Ellanden was on his back, staring up at his hands. Every now and then he'd snap his fingers beside his ear, making sure he could still hear it. The deafness had faded several hours before, but the memory of it still haunted him. He lifted his head with a vindictive glare.

"I'm sorry, Ash. Did you want some more *help*?"

The vampire grimaced apologetically, then gestured to the bars. Even gifted with immortal strength, he'd managed to make very little progress widening the crack from the knife on his own. The most he'd been able to do was budge it open a few more inches, but the rest of it held firm.

The fae glared a moment longer, then pushed to his feet with a sigh.

"You're weak and pathetic," he muttered, shoving the vampire aside to anchor his own strength against the cage. "The only reason I'm doing this is because you're so weak and pathetic."

"Got it," Asher murmured, bracing his hands alongside. "Weak and pathetic."

The two men dug in their heels, pushing with all their might. There was a metallic screech as the bars moved a few inches further. In a flash Cosette sprang up to help, pulling on the other side.

"The second this is over, we never speak to each other again," Ellanden panted, gritting his teeth with the strain. "Agreed?"

There was a deafening clang as one of the bars sprang open at last. Asher lit up in triumph, working it back and forth before popping it carefully back into place.

"Agreed."

The fae stared at him blankly. "You're putting it back? What was the point—"

"We can't have him see that it's broken. Otherwise, he'd only fix it."

Ellanden let out a frustrated sigh, running a hand through his hair. "And why let him fix it, when you're more than happy to oblige yourself..."

He trailed off when he realized the vampire was no longer listening. Asher's eyes had locked on the clouds of blood stained down the fae's neck. Ellanden wiped it irritably with the back of his sleeve, shooting a sharp glance in the process, and the vampire quickly lowered his eyes.

"This is going to work," he said quietly. "Just trust me."

As if on cue, there was a distant crash. The friends lifted their heads at the same time, listening to one crash blend into another as the giant stomped back to them through the forest.

"It had better," Ellanden murmured. "One way or another, we're about to find out."

THE DOOR BURST OPEN before any of them was ready, before they even had a chance to step away from the bars of the cage. Not that it mattered. The giant was in far better spirits than when he'd left them—probably something to do with the bruises and blood smeared across his face.

"I told you," he said smugly, without a hint of context. "I am stronger."

Hopefully that means there are a few fewer giants in the world...

Asher smiled warmly, nodding his head.

"Yes, I can see that now." He cocked his head once more to Ellanden. "My friend and I were just wondering which of us is stronger: a vampire or a fae."

Ellanden turned to him with a withering look.

Again? Really?!

"Actually," his hissed under his breath, "I was wondering why you keep picking *me* for all your precious little demonstrations."

The giant was too distracted to listen, staring down with a puzzled frown.

"I keep picking *you*," Asher murmured, "because of all the people here I figured *you'd* be the one most excited for a chance to kick my ass."

The fae considered for a moment, then turned to the giant with a radiant smile.

"That's right, we were," he announced, rolling up his sleeves. "I said it isn't that hard to beat a vampire, but Asher here disagrees."

There was a mighty creak as the giant stepped closer to the cage, examining them both with a tilt of his head. "Vampires are very strong...but fae are very strong."

Evie tried not to roll her eyes.

A brilliant assessment.

"It seems there's only one way to settle it," Freya piped in helpfully. "A fight to the death."

Both men glanced back in alarm, finding the *to the death* bit a tad extreme. But the giant's eyes lit up immediately, dancing with a feverish sort of glow.

"Yes—YES!"

Asher frowned thoughtfully, pretending to think it over.

"I guess it *is* the only way to settle things." His eyes flashed to Ellanden with the hint of a grin. "And who knows what might happen. I've been recently told that I'm pathetic and weak."

The fae smiled sweetly. "I bet there was a good reason for that. Come on then, vampire, hands up. We really haven't got all night—"

"Hang on." Asher shook his head, resting a tentative hand against the bars of the cage. "We can't do it in here. There isn't enough room. And what if one of the girls got hurt by accident?"

Evie stared at him a moment, then pushed to her feet with a hidden smile.

"What if you do it on the floor?" she asked innocently. "Plenty of room down there, though it might be too far down for our giant friend to see."

"He doesn't have to see," Cosette chimed in. "We can see it for ourselves and tell him what happened later."

The friends all vigorously approved this plan, but the giant's eyes had been darting between them—growing more and more frantic with each pass.

"No!" he finally shouted. "I will see! I will be the judge!"

Without further ado, he snapped the cage right off the chain and set it down in the middle of the table. The bars quaked precariously but held firm as the friends walked tentatively to the door.

"Yes," Asher said quietly, lips curved up in a secret smile, "this will do nicely."

The giant ripped open the door a second later, grabbing both men and dropping them onto the wooden slats. A moment later it shut again—sealing all three girls inside.

"Perfect!" he cried excitedly. "Now fight!"

The smiles faded slightly as the friends realized what was actually about to happen for the first time. The men had sparred many times before. Having grown up together, they'd even fought on occasion. But never had they raised their hands the way they'd be raising them now.

"So we're really doing this?"

Ellanden's voice was arrogant, almost mocking. But his eyes told an entirely different story, latching on to his friend's face as he desperately tried to intuit the plan.

"We're really doing it," Asher said with a hint of nerves. "Though I imagine it won't take that long. Just try to be careful." His eyes flickered to the heavy candle at the end of the table, a replacement for the lantern that had broken earlier. "We wouldn't want things getting out of hand."

Ellanden followed his gaze, paling with a little shiver. "No...we wouldn't."

Then the giant stomped his feet impatiently and they flew towards each other.

For as many times as Evie had imagined such a collision, she was completely unprepared when it happened now. Both men had been trained by their fathers, and fought with a skill that would have made the five kingdoms proud. But there were things working against them.

They loved each other like brothers. They didn't really want to hurt each other. And they were being watched by an unhinged giant who wouldn't be satisfied until he saw blood.

Lots of blood.

"Come on," Ellanden taunted, flipping backwards to avoid the vampire's attack before back-handing him across the face. "Don't hold back."

Asher suppressed a smile, spinning his body forward and catching the fae in a chokehold that could easily have snapped his neck. "I'm pretty sure you *want* me to hold back."

Ellanden's hands flew up to his arm. But instead of trying to pull himself loose he simply launched himself into the air, collapsing the vampire before landing lightly upon his back.

"I'm pretty sure I *don't*."

It was a magnificent display of talent, especially because there were few things more difficult than trying to make a fake fight look real. There was a breathtaking grace to how the fae moved, a kind of weightlessness that suggested the presence of wings. While the vampire ghosted around like liquid smoke—attacking and vanishing so quickly it was nearly impossible to fight back.

Unfortunately, a *fight* happened to be required.

"Not like that! REAL FIGHT!"

It soon became clear the tactics the men had been using weren't going to cut it. If there was one thing a giant knew, it was violence. He could tell when they were pulling their punches. He could tell when they would duck a second before a kick could land. Even when they sped things up, blurring so quickly around the table the princess had trouble keeping track, the giant's eyes followed along—seeing through their best intentions to the lie just underneath.

There was a little pause as each of them pulled back, panting softly and looking each other up and down. They'd been making good progress, but there was still a long way to go before they reached the edge of the table. It didn't help that every few minutes the giant had banged the wood in excitement and sent them flying right back to where they'd started.

Perhaps a little more force was required.

"All right," Ellanden said quietly, catching his breath, "a real fight." With no further warning, he whirled around and kicked the vampire right in the center of the chest. "I'd be delighted."

Asher flew backwards twenty feet, digging his fingers into the wood to stop the slide. A look of pure astonishment whitened his face as he lifted a hand to his bloodied chin.

"You'd be delighted," he repeated after summoning the breath to speak.

The fae smiled, slowly walking forward.

"Don't tell me it's never crossed your mind." He tilted his head appraisingly, spilling ivory hair to the other side. "Who'd *actually* win between us."

Asher pushed to his feet in one lithe movement. "I know who'd win between us," he said quietly.

Ellanden's smile faltered for the briefest moment, then hardened into something new. "Let's find out."

Evie pulled in a silent breath as they came together. This time was nothing like when they'd started. This time she could feel the impacts. See the drops of blood flying through the air.

The giant was delighted. She felt like she was going to be sick.

Faster and faster they moved, relying no longer upon tactics but pure muscle memory. One would swing, the other would duck. One would attack, the other would counter. An occasional gasp broke through, an occasional hiss or muffled cry. But aside from that, it was dead quiet.

Just get to the point, she thought nervously, fighting the urge to cover her eyes. *Just finish this.*

But it wasn't meant to be.

In a lot of ways, the fight was inevitable. Tensions had been brewing ever since the friends ventured down into the tunnel—unaware of the basilisk that lay waiting, that the vampire had forgotten the blood. They'd made up that night in the witch's cabin, vowed to put it all behind them. But try as she might, Evie could never forget the look on the vampire's face when he'd lost all sense of himself and decided to take the fae's blood.

She was willing to bet Ellanden couldn't forget it either.

She was willing to bet Ellanden was thinking about it right now.

There was a flash of white hair then the vampire let out a piercing cry, flying back at such speeds he almost fell off the side of the table. He took a moment to steady himself, spat a mouthful of blood, then slowly got to his feet, staring at his friend with an indecipherable expression.

"This isn't the time," he said quietly.

"Why not?" the fae countered, advancing once more. "As long as we're dancing..."

There was another cry, but this time the prince was the one who went flying. He flipped twice through the air, by no intention of his own, before falling hard onto the table.

"I thought this was over," Asher insisted, eyes dilating in spite of himself. "It was *done*."

"There was nothing for *you* to get over," Ellanden panted, pushing to his feet with a glare.

A cold hand closed around the princess' wrist.

"What are they talking about?" Cosette asked softly. "What haven't you said?"

Evie opened her mouth to answer, then stared helplessly through the bars. Of all the times for the moment to have come upon them, she couldn't think of anything worse.

"Over," Ellanden scoffed, shaking his head slowly. "What about just a few moments ago, when I saw you looking at my blood? *Again*." He flipped his hair back so the stains were clearly visible on the side of his neck, watching the vampire's reaction. "The wizard was right, wasn't he? You're never going to stop thinking about it. Just looking makes you want it all the more."

For a split second, Asher had no idea what to say.

Even though they were pounding each other to a pulp, he clearly hadn't expected the fae to ask the question so directly. Once it was in the open, it caught him completely unprepared. He knew how he wanted to answer. A part of him might have even believed that answer himself. But it was impossible to lie to a fae. Even more impossible to lie to his best friend. And the longer the words hung between them, the more his face heated with an incriminating flush of guilt.

Ellanden stared a long moment, then turned away. "That's what I thought."

At this point, the fight was basically over. The skill of two such opponents was a dangerous thing to leverage, and short of resorting to lethal harm there was no way either of them could win.

But there was still a job to be done. And the giant wasn't so easily satisfied.

"COME ON!" he shouted, pounding the table. "FIGHT!"

Asher slowly lifted his gaze, levelling him with a chilling glare. "I have a better idea," he said softly. "*Burn*."

Faster than sight, he ripped the broken bar off the cage and hurled it like a javelin straight towards the candle at the end of the table. The wax rattled precariously, tipping at the base, then gave way a second later when the fae streaked to the window and kicked it from behind.

In what felt like slow motion it fell onto the slats of wood, simultaneously igniting the kerosene that had spilled from the broken lantern just hours before. A second later, the entire table was ablaze. *And* the giant. *And* the little birdcage, from which the girls were still trying to escape.

"FIRE!" the giant shouted, like they were unable to see it for themselves. "FIRE!"

He jumped around like a maniac, slapping wildly at the flames crawling up his knees, while the boys doubled back to the cage—prying open the rest of the bars so the girls could slip through.

It only took seconds. And seconds were all they had.

From the moment the candle touched down, the world around them had burst into flame. Sizzling their skin and burning into their lungs as they grabbed each other and leapt into the open air.

"NO!" the giant cried. "Get BACK here!"

They might not have been dangling from the ceiling, but it was still a long way down. Each of the friends let out a painful cry as they smashed into the floor, lying dazed for a moment before forcing themselves up and racing full-tilt across the floor. Not surprisingly the giant beat them to it, but by now his mind was on other things. With a final cry, he abandoned the cabin altogether and kicked open the door—running full-speed to the garden pond.

The friends waited just long enough to him to run past before sprinting forward themselves. Leaning on each other for balance as they finally crossed the threshold, back into the real world.

The giant was soaking himself in the water. He never saw them melt noiselessly into the trees. It had been a brilliant plan, executed to fiery perfection.

There was only one problem.

The giant's screams hadn't been contained to their part of the forest. Neither had the sight of the blaze. Less than a minute after that candle had fallen over, the garden gate burst open and half a dozen other giants came rushing into the yard. They stopped in joint astonishment, staring at their companion who was still hitting patches of fire from his clothes.

"FIND THEM!" he bellowed. "DON'T LET THEM GET AWAY!"

The friends shrank into the greenery, staring with wide eyes as the giants scattered instantly through the garden, pulling up bushes and searching through the trees.

"How about it?" Evie whispered, grabbing Asher's sleeve. "Do you have a plan for *this*?"

"Yeah," he breathed, watching as the monsters came closer. "...run!"

Chapter 4

The good thing about being chased by giants: you could always hear them coming.

The bad thing about being chased by giants: ...you were being chased by giants.

The friends kept to their hiding place for only a moment before those thundering boots got too close and they were forced to retreat, lest they be crushed beneath them. It was a dangerous ploy, but instead of scattering as they did before they stuck close together—keeping tight hold of each other as they moved quickly and silently through the dense underbrush.

It was a slow process, especially because giants' eyes had accustomed themselves to detect even the slightest bit of movement. When a creature stood sixty feet above the world around them, picking up on those little things was often their best chance at capturing their prey.

As if they needed another advantage.

The princess bit back a scream as a massive shadow hovered over her, temporarily blocking out the sun. At first she thought it was their old captor, then she realized it was only his shoe. It dropped out of nowhere, crashing to the ground before she had time to move. Only a decade's worth of training gave her the edge she needed to leap away in time. Even then, she was yanked immediately backwards as the toe of his boot caught the edge of her cloak.

Evie!

She didn't know whether Asher had actually said the word, or if he was simply screaming inside his head that loud. Either way, their eyes met for a split second before she was pulled to the ground. She didn't know whether or not the giant had seen her. From the second her face hit the grass, she'd been too afraid to lift her eyes. It was perhaps the only thing that saved her life.

While she might not have been able to see the giant, the faces of her friends were perfectly clear. All four of them were crouched safely in the underbrush, hidden from sight, but each one shared the same look of terror. No, the giant obviously hadn't seen her yet. But yes, he would the second she moved. Of course, if she didn't move...

I'm going to die here, she thought with a gasp. *He's going to step on me.*

...he probably won't even know.

Oddly enough, the second part bothered her almost as much as the first. It was one thing to go out fighting a giant in a blaze of glory, but it was quite another to become some faceless after-thought forever smeared on the bottom of his shoe.

As she lay there hyperventilating, a silent struggle was going on just beneath the leaves.

"Let me go," Asher hissed, straining frantically against the imprisoning grip of the fae. "I need to get over there—let me go!"

"AND NO EATING!" the giant called suddenly, remembering he'd given only partial instructions. "THEY ARE STILL MINE!"

The men stared up at him for a moment before returning to their desperate battle.

"You go out there now—he'll see you and kill her," Ellanden muttered, straining against the effort of holding the vampire against his will. The only thing making it remotely possible was that Cosette was standing right alongside. "No movement. It's the only chance she has."

Asher's face tightened in resignation, though his feet were still angled in the grass.

"I can't just watch," he panted breathlessly. "I can't just—"

But in that moment, several things happened at once.

There was a shout from the other side of the garden. The giant in question whirled around in surprise. Evie went flying backwards as her cloak finally came free…

…and landed in the vampire's arms.

The friends fell down like dominos. Even Freya, who hadn't been connected to the rest, was too close to avoid the collision. They landed in a pile beneath a flowering laurel, trying desperately to keep quiet as they peered up through the leaves.

Sure enough, the giant was leaving.

But their flight toward freedom had only just begun.

"On three," Ellanden breathed as they pushed to their feet. He pulled in a breath, about to begin the countdown, when the ferns in front of them suddenly parted and they found themselves in the spotlight once more. "*Three!*"

IT WAS LIKE SOMETHING out of a dream. More terrifying than the princess could have imagined.

No sooner would they evade one giant than another would rise up in its place. No one saw them directly—a fact that repeatedly saved their lives—but there were only so many close calls a group of people could sustain before they began to lose people along the way.

It had almost happened already.

Freya had just begun to scramble over a fallen tree trunk when the entire thing got kicked sideways, sending her flying into the air. Ellanden was almost crushed to death when a giant took an unexpected step backwards but Asher streaked out of nowhere, tackling him around the waist.

The two men tumbled across the grass, trying to slow the momentum of the fall. When they finally came to a stop, Ellanden blinked twice then shoved the vampire's arm away from him.

Whether it was a belated reflex from their fight or something else, they would never know.

"This isn't going to work," Cosette whispered, eyes flickering around the grass as they re-joined the others. "They'll catch us long before we're free of this garden. We need a new plan."

The others wanted to argue, it felt like suicide to stop moving, but the fae was right. The rest of the forest was perfectly silent, the search was narrowing, and they needed another way. Instead of looking around they turned their gaze upward, staring into the canopy of trees.

"What do you think?" Evie whispered, not needing to say the words out loud.

The boys nodded slowly, already of the same mind.

"That could work," Ellanden murmured, "but it's a long climb in the open before we get to the cover of that first branch."

At that point, Freya realized what they were talking about for the first time.

"Are you guys crazy?!" she hissed. "You want to put us at biting height?! They won't even have to lift us to their mouths, they can just lean forward!"

"It's better than getting trampled to death," Cosette whispered, tugging on her arm.

The witch resisted, *fiercely*. "No—it actually isn't!" Her eyes flickered again to the towering redwood before she dug her feet firmly into the mud. "I'm not going up there. There's not a chance in—"

Ellanden swung her over his shoulder, sprinting with the others towards the trunk.

"—seven hells!"

She banged uselessly on his back. She even debated firing a volley of sparks, but it was sure to draw attention. That being said, if that spotlight could be shifted somewhere else...

"Hang on," she gasped suddenly. "Lift me a little higher!"

By now, they'd reached the base of the tree. The fae had been in the process of removing the witch from his shoulder, but stopped when she grabbed a fistful of his hair.

"Freya, we've got to keep moving—"

"Just a little higher," she insisted. Their eyes met for a brief moment as the giants ripped up the garden just beyond. "Trust me. They're attracted to movement, right? Then we need a little diversion."

He gave her a bracing look, then wrapped his hands around her legs and lifted her onto his shoulders. Ironically enough, it was the same way he'd carried her through the forest as a child.

"Whatever you're doing—do it quickly."

She nodded hastily, gazing out over the woodland glen.

It was hard to see much of anything past the giants rampaging through the trees, but amidst the chaos she managed to catch sight of a tiny flutter of wings.

"Perfect."

With precision aim she sent a shiver of golden light through the underbrush, hitting a bush on the far side. In a flash the air exploded with dozens of butterflies, clouding skyward in a burst of confusion, sunlight glinting off the colorful patterns as they swirled towards the heavens.

The giants turned at the same time, drawn by all the movement, allowing the friends the split second they needed to scramble up the base of the tree. At least...that was the plan.

The princess lodged one foot after the other, digging her fingers into the bark as her long cloak fluttered in the breeze. There was a reason these kinds of things were supposed to be done in the daylight, with branches and other things to help you along. Fit as she was, trained as she was, there simply was no way to scramble up the unending trunk of an evergreen tree.

Both of the fae were already on the nearest branch, having simply sprinted upward with that infuriating natural grace. Freya was making good progress, but no sooner had Ellanden settled himself than he dove right back down—lifting the young woman straight off the bark and swinging her onto his back. Her arms and legs tightened as she leaned down with a roguish grin.

"Be honest...is this flirting?"

He actually slipped a bit in surprise, throwing a quick glance behind him. One look at her teasing face and he began climbing again, laughing quietly as he went.

"You are *completely* deranged."

The princess was making good progress behind them, but the soon-to-be-famous butterfly defense would only buy them so much time. She doubled her speed, trying to tap into some of that elusive shifter strength, when a pair of cool fingers wrapped around her wrists.

There was a blur of fiery hair as the world vanished. A moment later, she was on the branch.

Her cheeks flushed as she cast a sideways look at the vampire—the one who was staring out into the garden as if he hadn't done a thing. If it weren't for the clan of giants intent on eating them, the whole thing might have been funny. As it stood, she couldn't resist poking him in the ribs.

"Keep your hands to yourself."

They said it at the same time, then turned to each other with a little smile. It might have been the bond—the princess had yet to even wrap her head around that one. But somehow, she didn't think so. The two had been finishing each other's sentences since they were just five years old.

"So I was thinking..." she began tentatively, watching as the giants circled the grass, "if we make it through this—"

"I know," he interrupted with a quiet sigh. "We need to talk."

She looked at him in surprise, unable to resist a smile.

In the last few days, they'd been tracked across a frozen tundra by a pack of undead leopards, fallen off a cliff, captured by a giant, only to narrowly escape setting themselves on fire.

Yet through all that...it seemed the vampire had something else on his mind.

"I was *going* to say," she continued, "I'm banning all bird cages in the High Kingdom."

He shot a glance at her face, unable to tell if she was joking, then froze with sudden tension as the giants' search party came to an abrupt halt. The largest of the group—the one who'd been holding them prisoner—stared around the garden before throwing up his hands with a roar.

"How did this HAPPEN?!" How are they GONE?!"

The friends shrank farther beneath the cover of the branches, watching as the other giants shifted around uneasily. Most of them seemed more concerned with the fiery demolition of their companion's cabin than with the loss of whatever occupants might have been inside. Given the average attention span of a giant, Evie could only imagine how long such a thing must have taken to build. Only the tallest of the group, the one who'd demanded his share of the leopard, seemed to share his friend's frustration—perhaps thinking there was a tiny royal snack involved.

"We split up?" he suggested. "Search the rest of the woods?"

It was a stupid plan, even for a giant. Once they were through the gate and back in the outside world, there would be little chance of finding them. Hiding places were endless, and that was if the giants picked the right direction to start looking and the friends didn't simply run away.

That's what made it so bloody difficult to stay put in a tree. *Hoping* they wouldn't be seen.

The giant who'd caught them seemed to agree. His face tightened angrily, before crumbling at the same time. "Can't find them in woods...they need to be here." In a bizarre coincidence, the giant let out a sigh and actually leaned against the very tree in which they were hiding. He was so close, Katerina could see the grizzled coils of hair sticking out of his ear. "Good little pets..."

Again, the giants shared a bewildered glance. A savage breed by nature, they respected only those things too powerful to kill. The giant in question clearly met the criteria. And yet he lived in a cabin, not a cave. He read books and tried to domesticate the locals. The brute was a paradox.

"There's more leopard," one of them offered hesitantly. "If you want something to eat."

The others nodded enthusiastically, several pointing up toward the cliffs.

"...was never going to eat them," the giant mumbled, unheard by the others. "Only wanted a friend..."

Evie's heart softened with a stab of sympathy as she remembered the giant's lonely fireside, the look of peaceful contentment on his face as he drifted off to sleep. Her eyes tightened—

Then fingers dug into her arm.

"Don't you *dare* feel sorry for him," Ellanden mouthed.

She blushed, and pulled her arm away.

"We check the forest anyway?" another giant offered.

There was a mighty sigh, then the one who'd captured them shook his head, staring back at the remains of his cabin with a wistful regret. "No, we head to the snow...kill more kitties."

The others seemed to think this was a *great* idea. The friends embraced it with open arms. It could have been a rather peaceful end to a volatile chapter of the gang's history.

But, as usual, fate had other plans.

As he was leaving, the giant sighed once more in frustration—pounding his fist against the base of the tree. The evergreen rattled violently, quaking from its roots to the tips of its leaves. The ground was quaking below it, and a second later Evie fell silently off the branch into the open air.

The next few seconds felt like slow motion.

She remembered her hair flying up in front of her, blocking everything else from sight. She remembered the giant paused beneath her, unaware his little prize was about to land right on top of his head. And she remembered a hand reaching out to grab her and staring up into a pair of dark eyes.

He couldn't risk losing her. He wouldn't dream of letting go.

When the giant ran off with his kinsmen a second later, he simply jumped off the branch himself. Falling with her this time and then landing lightly upon the forest floor, with the princess cradled safely in his arms.

She stared up at him in wonder, feeling his pounding heartbeat echo in her own chest. All those years, it had been there all along. She didn't know how she'd missed it.

"Ash—"

He kissed her.

Without thought. Without hesitation. Without an ounce of regret.

He just kissed her.

A second later, she was kissing him back.

There was a quiet rustling as the others friends landed beside them. They didn't notice. They didn't even pull back for breath until a throat cleared awkwardly, and they twisted their heads to find themselves staring into another pair of dark, eternal eyes.

Ellanden opened his mouth to speak, then closed it once again. A childhood dynamic subtly changed. The chaotic clearing went quiet as the three friends stared in silence.

Then Freya bounded up beside them with a beaming smile.

"Well, *there's* something you don't see every day..."

Chapter 5

"Landi—can you wait up for a second?"

The fae continued moving at a steady pace, leading them through the trees. Since escaping the giant's lair the friends had been moving fast in the opposite direction, casting occasional looks over their shoulders, listening carefully all the while. The fae had been speaking just as quickly, keeping up a breathless one-way stream of conversation, planning out their next few steps on the fly.

It might have been making up for lost time. It might have been something else.

"...obviously didn't account for the giants, but it's like Cosette said: a lot has changed in the last ten years." He stopped abruptly in his tracks, glanced at the sun, then made a slight alteration to their course. "That being said, the geography itself isn't different. As long as we continue heading due west we'll eventually reach the river, which will lead us down to the sea..."

The princess stared at the back of his head, then continued walking up the trail.

While the fae had yet to stop talking, there was a lot he didn't say. And strangely enough, she didn't think it was the brush with a giant, the fight with his best friend, or even their subsequent fiery escape from an over-sized birdcage that weighed heaviest on his mind.

"...benefits of taking a larger ship, but at this point anonymity might beat speed..."

Since the friends were children, people had thought their relationship was a bit strange.

Three enchanting immortals, living in such close proximity? Studying with the same tutors, drinking at the same parties, sleeping under the same stars? How could they *just* be friends?

But since they were children, the friends had laughed those rumors away.

It was something they had never questioned. As natural as taking a breath. When you grew up with each other as family, you thought of each other as family. It was as simple as that.

There were no barriers between them, no secrets they hadn't shared.

They sat together at funerals, handled each other's break-ups, held back each other's hair after a night of drinking. They had provided each other with enough outrageous alibies that, as a rule, no one at the castle believed a single word they had to say.

It was the friendship that sustained them. The eternal communion of three kindred spirits.

...and we just shattered that all to hell.

"—really just a matter of what kind of wood they've used for the hull. If we're talking about something hard like oak, then it could probably navigate the passage in a few days. But there's this certain kind of Odesian cedar that's actually—"

She bowed her head with a sigh, glancing sideways at Asher instead.

The two hadn't spoken to each other since leaving the garden. Both had effectively shut down the second they walked through the gate. It wasn't that either of them regretted what had happened. Quite the contrary, the princess found herself in a dreamy kind of shock. It simply wasn't something either of them knew how to discuss. Let alone in front of the others. Let alone having recently escaped a clan of giants with little clouds of smoke still rising from their backs.

The vampire was walking silently beside her, keeping his eyes on the ground.

Unlike the princess, who occasionally tried to interject, he'd made no attempt to disrupt the fae's monologue. He simply trailed at the back of the group with a thoughtful expression, listening with quiet patience to whatever Ellanden had to say.

He'd shot his fair share of looks at the princess, not that she'd seen a single one. He'd even debated pulling her aside so they could speak in private. But for the most part his head was back in that garden, replaying what had happened again, and again, and again...

"—*larch* is what you really want. But that's incredibly difficult to find. It's only at certain elevations that you can even—"

"Ellanden!" the princess called, finally incensed. "Can we talk for a second?"

He glanced over his shoulder, looking surprised she'd even ask. "We're talking about ships," he replied.

"One of us is doing that," Freya muttered under her breath. "One of us is considering setting the fae on fire."

Evie clenched her jaw, stomping past the rest to join him at the front.

"Yeah, as fascinating as all that is—I *really* need to speak with you." Her eyes narrowed as she struggled to keep pace. "Call me crazy, but I get the feeling something might be wrong."

"What do you mean?" The fae held back a heavy branch for the others, releasing it before Asher had a chance to make it through. "Everything's fine."

The princess gave him a measured look, then raised her voice. "We're setting up camp."

The rest of them stopped at once, Ellanden glancing around in genuine surprise.

"Right now? Evie, we can keep going another few hours—"

"No," she said shortly, "we can't." With a defiant *plop* she dropped her cloak onto the ground between them, perching on the rock beside it. "Cosette, why don't you see what you can scrounge up for dinner? Freya, why don't you go with her? Moral support."

Translation: get the heck out of here.

The girls couldn't nod fast enough. Tension had been building ever since their daring escape into the woods, and they had no intention of being there when things finally boiled over.

"Do you have any preferences?" Freya asked lightly as they backed into the woods. "We could try to get some rabbits, or maybe a nice ferret—"

Cosette grabbed her hand a moment later, quickly dragging her out of sight.

For the first time since emerging from the wizard's cave, the three friends found themselves suddenly alone. Most days, it would have been a blessing. Today, it most certainly was not.

Evie stared at Ellanden. Ellanden stared at Evie. Asher stared at the ground in between them, wondering why the princess had insisted upon getting the three of them alone.

There was a split second of silence, then everyone started talking all at once.

"Look, this really isn't—"

"We really don't have to—"

"I'm sorry you saw the two of us kiss!"

The men turned as one to stare at the princess.

As usual, they'd been of exactly the same mind. Hoping to simply ignore what had happened until one or both felt comfortable sweeping it under the rug. It was a passive-aggressive compartmentalization method they were proud to have perfected over the course of their young lives.

The princess was a bit more direct.

"I'm sorry you saw the two of us kiss," she said again, a little breathless this time. "It's not how I would have told you. It had never even happened before today. It's not like..." She caught herself, feeling suddenly unsure. "It's not like we were trying to keep it from you or something—"

"*That's* what you think this is about?" Ellanden asked incredulously, stopping the discussion in its tracks. "*That's* why you think I've been angry?"

She froze uncertainly, mind going blank. "...it isn't?"

The fae glanced up at the canopy of trees, trying hard to rein in his temper. It wasn't exactly his strong suit, but when he looked back a moment later he was strangely calm.

"I could give a crap that you guys kissed."

If it was possible, the princess was even more baffled than before. She shot a quick look at Asher, who was staring warily at the prince, before turning back in complete astonishment.

"...really?"

Ellanden took one look at their faces and broke down in spite of himself, letting out a quiet laugh as he raked his fingers through his hair.

"I mean, it's a little weird, but...I'd never be angry that you kissed."

Then, what? Evie thought desperately. The fight? That would certainly make sense, except that I wasn't a part of the fight and he hasn't been speaking to me either—

"You know about the bond," Asher said quietly.

The two men locked eyes. Then Ellanden nodded.

"I was standing right there," he said softly, glancing at Evie as well. "I was literally holding Asher steady when your blood splashed into his face." His eyes tightened at the memory before resting on each of his friends. "Were you guys just not going to tell me?"

Evie grabbed his hands without thinking, both horrified and relieved at the same time.

"Of course not!" she exclaimed. "Of course we were going to tell you!"

The fae lifted his eyebrows slowly, wanting very much to believe that was true.

"We were in that cage for almost three days," he began tentatively. "We were camped out on the tundra a full day before that. I kept waiting for one of you to say something, but—"

"I didn't know how," Evie interrupted, feeling suddenly bereft. "I...I still don't."

"We haven't talked about it yet ourselves," Asher added quietly, glancing between them. "I never meant for it to happen—you guys know how I feel about that sort of thing. It just caught me by surprise and I don't..."

He forced himself to look at the princess for the first time.

"...I don't know what it means."

She let out a quiet sigh.

Yeah, me neither.

Time seemed to suspend as they stared at each other.

There was finally nothing chasing them. They were finally alone. But now that the moment was upon them, neither of them could think of a single way to break that unending silence.

Ellanden glanced between them, then folded his arms with a little grin. "Sounds like you two have a lot to talk about, huh?"

They stared a moment longer, then turned to him at the same time. Far from leaving the fae had settled in, leaning back on the grass as he stared up at them with an expectant smile.

It took Evie a second to realize what was happening, then her eyes narrowed with a withering glare. "And you're staying right there, are you?"

He glanced between them with a look of total innocence. "I just assumed any conversation would include me."

The princess' fingers curled into automatic fists, but the vampire grabbed her swiftly by the arm and took her away, leading her deeper into the woods.

THEY WALKED A COMICALLY long time without speaking, effectively leaving the campsite and everyone in it behind. The setting sun, which had been hovering stubbornly above the trees, finally slipped beneath the horizon—cloaking the forest in darkness as they continued on their way.

Every so often they'd glance at each other, silently panic, then continue onward. It had gotten to the point where Evie was afraid they'd left what Ellanden had called the 'Middle Country' behind. Then, all at once, the vampire came to a sudden stop in front of her.

Finally, he's ready to—

She trailed off as her eyes flickered a few feet past him. No, he wasn't ready to talk. The two of them had simply walked themselves to the edge of a cliff.

...well, that's ironic.

Her body froze in surprise as a sudden smile crept up the side of her face. She bit her lip, trying to keep Asher from seeing, but it got harder and harder the longer they stood there. Instead of seeing the humor, the vampire looked like he was having some kind of panic attack. His dark eyes kept flickering over the side of the bluff like he was honestly trying to find a way down.

"Should have brought some rope," he murmured under his breath.

That did it.

A second later, the princess burst out laughing. The kind of long, uncontrolled laughing that took one's breath away and only stopped when it was ready. The kind that was impossibly contagious, no matter how hard one might try to resist.

Asher tried hard. He was not successful.

His hands ran over his face as he took a deliberate step away from the cliff, shaking silently. All the more so when the ground where he'd just been standing crumbled into the abyss. The two were still going strong when they left it all behind, settling in a little clearing among the trees.

For the first time in what felt like ages, things felt natural between them. Reclining on a patch of moonlit grass, stretched out side by side as they stared up at the stars. How many times had they lain in exactly this position? How many nights had they drifted peacefully off to sleep?

When things finally quieted down, they made no effort to move. They simply nestled closer together, legs touching, smiles still lingering on their faces. Asher's arm lifted invitingly and she slid automatically underneath, curling into his side, resting her head on his chest.

It was quiet for a while. Then all at once, his body stiffened.

"I felt this way before the bond," he blurted.

She froze in surprise, slowly twisting her head to look at him. Never before had she seen such an expression. He was completely vulnerable, laying everything on the line.

"I...I've felt this way for a long time," he admitted softly. "For a lot longer than I knew myself." He blushed suddenly, lowering his eyes. "I've wanted to kiss you for even longer."

The princess stared up at him in the darkness. She wanted to reassure him, to take his hand and promise that she felt the same way. But all she could do was stare, completely spellbound.

"So why didn't you?"

His eyes flashed to hers, resting there for a while before he shrugged with a sad smile.

"Because it was you."

Some people might have been offended, lost themselves in a tailspin of misinterpretation and self-doubt, but Evie knew exactly what he meant. How many times had she peeked at him from the corner of her eye, thinking exactly the same thing? That this beautiful dark-haired boy wasn't hers to love as anything more than a friend. That they'd been through too much together. That there wasn't a chance in hell he could possibly feel the same.

Without stopping to think she rolled onto his chest, tendrils of crimson hair spilling down his arms. They stared at each other for a long moment, feeling a bit like they were right back on the edge of that cliff, then she leaned down and kissed him.

For the first time since setting off on their grand adventure...time was on their side.

It started as something sweet, a gentle caress so exquisitely tender the feel of it brought tears to the princess' eyes. His hand slipped into her hair, their faces angling naturally together as the light of the moon glowed silver upon their skin. Then it started to dawn on them that they were truly alone.

And kissing wasn't nearly enough.

The temperature between them spiked as his body arched off the grass, taking her along with him. Her legs wrapped around his waist and the fingers laced in her hair tightened into a sudden fist, anchoring their faces together. His lips coaxed hers open, his tongue slipping into her mouth. Her heartbeat raced, and before she knew what she was doing she'd yanked his shirt right over his head.

It fell in the grass behind them. Her fingers started struggling with the clasp on his pants.

Then his hand closed gently over hers.

"Evie."

His voice stopped her frantic efforts, soothing the fire racing through her veins.

For a second, she was almost too overwhelmed to look at him. The world was sharpening back into focus, and she was suddenly aware that her legs were hitched firmly around his waist.

"What's the matter?" she whispered, afraid to meet his eyes. "Don't you want to?"

A pair of cool fingers slipped beneath her chin. She pulled away instinctively, but when she finally lifted her head he was staring down with a tender smile.

"Of course I want to," he said softly. "I told you, I've wanted to for a long time." He paused a moment, staring at her in the moonlight. "But you've never done this before."

Her cheeks flamed as she dropped her eyes to the ground.

Both of her friends were...experienced. That was a generous way of putting it. Since he was fourteen years old Ellanden had been sneaking off to the stables with the nymph of the moment, and Asher had always been too attractive for his own good. Women noticed. They noticed back.

The only one who hadn't crossed that particular line was the princess herself.

"I know I'm not as practiced as some of the girls you've been with," she mumbled, eyes locked on the forest floor. "But I could try to—"

"Seven hells, Everly!" Asher interrupted. "That's not what I meant!"

He shifted her slightly so she was sitting on his lap instead of straddling it, still staring affectionately into her eyes. When she refused to look at him, he simply waited. When she finally conceded with a petulant glare, a little smile was twinkling in his eyes.

"My wrist is broken," he said quietly, stroking back a lock of her hair. "The fae cracked three of my ribs. I'm not exactly at my best, we're in the middle of the forest, and there's a decent chance you have a mild concussion from when that giant smashed you into the ground."

Evie considered this for a moment. "Well, everybody's got problems..."

He pulled her closer with a laugh, pressing a tender kiss to the top of her head. "I'm saying, this isn't how you want your first time."

Perhaps she should have been embarrassed—that flaming blush had yet to leave her cheeks. If it had been anyone else saying it she probably would have fled the woods, never to return again.

But as it stood...she was sincerely touched.

"I want it to be perfect," he murmured, flashing a sudden grin. "Ideally, I want it to be with me..." They laughed quietly before he stroked a lock of hair from her face. "But seriously, Evie, I don't want you to regret anything. I want it to be exactly what you deserve."

She stared at him a moment longer, then nodded. Two fingers started walking teasingly up his bare chest as a little smile played around her lips.

"So that's it? You're blowing me off?"

He laughed a little breathlessly.

"Yeah, that's *totally* what I'm doing." He glanced down at her fingers, adjusting himself with a bit of strain. "You don't make it easy."

She shrugged casually, raking a nail down the center of his chest. He shivered in spite of himself, trying to fight back every screaming impulse, then caught her face between gentle hands. Their eyes locked for a fleeting moment as his thumbs swept lightly across her cheeks.

"But it'll be worth it."

Her eyes warmed and she stopped her shameless teasing. She kissed him softly instead. "Yes, it will."

The two shared a secret smile.

"In the meantime...I'll just try to control myself."

He reached behind him for his shirt, but she beat him to it—dangling it casually out of reach. His eyes sparkled as he leaned back on his elbows, letting her enjoy the view.

"This hardly seems fair."

"This was your choice," she said loftily, soaking it all in. "I wanted to keep going. You had the brilliant idea of controlling yourself. How's that going, by the way?"

His teeth sank into his lower lip, fighting back a grin. "You tell me."

It was a cruel trick, but vampires weren't exactly known for fighting fair. And looking at him now, reclining half-naked in the grass, the princess couldn't imagine being able to stop.

The man was sheer perfection.

It was as if he'd been carved by a master, every part of him designed to entrance. From the long sculpted lines of his body, to the waves of onyx hair falling gracefully to his chin, right down to those dark hypnotic eyes that seemed to hook somewhere deep inside her, pulling her ever closer.

Bathed in the silver light of the moon, he looked like the kind of fantasy you'd stumble upon in a dream rather than something that could actually happen in real life.

Evie blinked twice, aware that he was still waiting for an answer to his question.

"It's going fine," she said quickly, feeling a little light-headed. "Here—take your shirt."

He pulled it over his head with a grin, sliding his arms gracefully into the sleeves before pulling her right back down in the grass beside him, curled contentedly against his chest. They lay in silence for a while, gazing up at the stars. Then she peered up with a little smile.

"How would it be?"

"What do you mean?"

Her eyes twinkled with mischief as she twisted around to see him better. "My first time—how would it be?"

He glanced at her in surprise, then softened with a thoughtful smile. "It would be...whatever you wanted." His eyes swept briefly around the clearing, dancing at the thought. "It could be in a place not unlike this one, only at a better time. I'd take you out for a midnight picnic. Get you drunk. Hide your clothes. Demand payment for a ride back to the castle."

She snorted with laughter, pressing her face to his chest. "So *that's* what you meant by perfect."

"Perfect for me," he clarified. "I don't really care how it is for you."

"Good to know."

His arms tightened as he pressed a gentle kiss to her cheek. It was quiet for a while longer, then he glanced down with sudden curiosity. "Have you ever thought about it? How you'd want it to be?"

Yes.

"I was thinking right in the middle of a battle," she deflected easily, flipping around so they were gazing up at the same starry sky. "Poised for victory, soaked in blood."

"Soaked in blood," he echoed with a grin. "Are you trying to turn me on?"

"We'd meet somewhere up on the battlements, our wounds would be mysteriously healed, our armor would be miraculously gone..."

She was about to go further, when the smile suddenly faded from her face. All at once, the fantasy was a bit too real. All at once, it demanded some answers of its own.

"Ash...what about the fae?"

"The fae is most definitely *not* invited," he said decisively.

"I'm serious," she murmured, easing off his chest. "Your shoulder is messed up, and you have a broken wrist. How were you even able to do all that with three cracked ribs?"

He propped up on his elbows, surprised by the sudden shift in tone. "Well, you happened to provide some excellent motivation—"

"*Asher*," she admonished, stopping the banter in its tracks. "What are you doing to do about Ellanden?"

The vampire stared at her a second more before suddenly turning away. His knees pulled up to his chest as he gazed out at the moonlit horizon. Then he bowed his head with a quiet sigh.

"I almost took his life, Everly. I choked him out, yanked back his neck, and almost drained the life right out of him. And he's right," he added dejectedly. "...I think about it all the time."

Evie stared down at the silver grass, remembering each moment as if it were burned into her head. The way he'd lifted the broken prince off the ground, sweeping back his hair. The way he'd pulled back at the last minute and strangled him instead, just so he wouldn't see it coming.

It was unforgivable. But the friends were immortal. They'd be together for a long time.

"You need to find a way to fix it," she said simply.

The vampire shook his head, as if she was asking the impossible. But she lay a steady hand on his arm, forcing him to look into her eyes.

"Ash...you need to find a way."

He held her gaze for a moment, then nodded with a sigh. "Yeah...I guess I do."

Chapter 6

By the time Evie and Asher got back to camp the fae had already made a crude sort of shelter. And the girls had already returned from their excursion into the forest—their pockets laden down with roots and berries, as well as a rabbit Cosette apparently killed with her bare hands.

"—it was *disgusting*," Freya was saying, recreating the moment with such ghoulish hand gestures even Ellanden was fighting back a grimace. "And when the thing screamed—" She caught herself suddenly, lighting up with a bright smile. "Oh, hey guys! Have a good chat?"

The fae glanced over his shoulder, then gestured wordlessly to the makeshift camp. "Congratulations, you arrived in time to miss all the work."

Evie flashed a grin, walking up beside him to examine what he'd done. Given how few supplies had survived the leopard attack, much less the kidnapping that had followed, it was rather impressive. Devoid of anything more than a simple cutting knife, the fae had managed to strip the branches from a nearby tree and weave them into a seamless canopy which he'd draped over an out-cropping of rocks. A blazing fire was roaring just a few feet away, throwing off beams of light.

"Not bad," she said appreciatively, warming her hands by the flames. "Of course, I would have preferred something with a view..."

"That's no problem," he said generously. "You can sleep outside."

They shared a quick grin as the girls settled down beside them. Freya was happily eating the entire group's ration of berries. Cosette was looking vaguely traumatized as she wiped blood and bits of fur from her hands. Only the vampire kept his distance, staring at the fae appraisingly, taking the princess' words of advice to heart. Of course, Ellanden remained predictably oblivious.

"Before you two decided to grace us with your presence, we were discussing the best way to barter for passage on a ship," he said distractedly, hacking off another evergreen branch and weaving it skillfully in with the rest. "Since we have nothing to trade and we're running low on coin I figured we could organize a little robbery, try to steal some horses."

Evie lifted her eyebrows, and Asher stepped forward with a grin.

"That's your big idea? Make us horse thieves?"

Do they still hang people for that? I feel like they always hang people for that.

The fae nodded soundly, planning as he went. "They'd speed up the journey through the lowlands, then we could sell them for safe passage the second we got to shore. It wouldn't be hard to take them. We'd only need five." He caught himself suddenly, throwing the vampire an innocent look. "Or maybe you two could share."

The princess blushed furiously, but the vampire only smiled—ducking under the tree branch as his hands began working from the other side. "Is that how it's going to be?"

Ellanden continued weaving, nodding all the while. "That's how it's going to start, yeah."

Asher grinned faintly, taking the bait. "And what happens next?"

The fae shrugged, as if what happened next was inevitable. "Eventually, I realize I'm not okay with it after all and you guys are forced to break up."

The girls looked up in unison, but Asher nodded briskly.

"That seems fair."

He watched as the fae finished with what he was doing, pressing the last of the branches into place. It wasn't until he started walking away that Asher caught his arm, lowering his voice quietly.

"Ellanden—"

The fae pulled back reflexively, shaking his head with a tight smile.

"We were only doing what we had to. The giant said to fight," Asher said.

A casual dismissal, but there was a bit more to it than that.

"I'm serious," Asher pressed softly. "Could we—"

Then all at once Ellanden came back, closing the distance in just a few steps. His eyes locked on the vampire's collar, lingering a moment before tightening in an unfamiliar kind of rage.

"Actually, yeah—let's talk."

Before Asher could answer, he grabbed him fiercely by the arm—dragging him away from the camp and into the trees. The girls stared after them in silence, frozen exactly where they'd stood.

After a few seconds, Freya glanced at the others. "So they're finally going to kill each other?"

Cosette's eyes tightened with a hint of worry. "Yeah, I guess so."

Not if I have anything to do with it...

Evie flashed them both a quick smile and gestured towards the woods. "I'm just going to...check on something completely unrelated."

She was gone a moment later, sprinting full speed into the trees.

BOTH OF THE MEN THE princess was tracking could be as silent as ghosts, but it didn't take long to find them. Mostly because they were shouting at the top of their lungs.

"I cannot *believe* you!"

There was a faint scuffling sound as Evie slipped noiselessly into the underbrush, staring at a little clearing in the woods. Ellanden was pacing furiously back and forth, throwing occasional death looks over his shoulder. Asher stood frozen, as frustrated as he was confused.

Guess there's no reason to worry about the giants hearing us. We managed to escape that danger... and find our way into a whole new territory of trouble.

"Can't believe *what*?" he demanded, not for the first time. "Look, I'll admit you have plenty of reasons to be angry with me, but you're going to have to narrow it down."

"Don't give me that!" Ellanden fired back. "You know exactly what you've done!"

For a split second, the princess was afraid the fight was going to start all over again. They didn't need a giant egging them on. They could carry on destroying each other all by themselves.

But this wasn't your usual argument. And it wasn't your usual rage. Instead of throwing a punch Ellanden paced back across the clearing, lowering his voice with a dangerous kind of calm.

"You have a broken wrist."

The vampire glanced down, thrown by the sudden shift in momentum. "Yeah, I...I remember it happening."

Evie grimaced involuntarily. She remembered, too. The fae had done it himself, snapping it neatly behind the vampire's back before launching him across the length of the giant's table. Even trapped in a cage on the other side, the princess could swear she'd heard it crack.

But Ellanden wasn't looking for absolution. He was absolutely incensed.

"You've also got a messed-up shoulder," he continued in that same deadly voice, "probably a couple of cracked ribs..."

Asher shook his head warily, trying to follow along. "Why are you—"

"And what about Everly?" the fae demanded. "Did you think of that? What about the tear in her ankle, the lacerations that are still healing on her back?" He closed the distance between them, standing toe to toe. "What about the fact that she probably has a concussion from when that giant smashed her into the ground? Did you think about *any* of that?"

Asher stared back at him in amazement, while Evie was simply stunned.

She'd had no idea the fae had been monitoring her injuries so closely, especially considering his own were infinitely more severe. Despite the tension radiating through the clearing, she found herself sincerely touched. But there was an admonishment in the prince's voice she didn't understand. A protective censure buried beneath all those layers of rage.

Then all at once...she noticed what Ellanden had apparently seen back at the campsite.

Asher had left properly clothed. He'd returned with his shirt on backwards.

Seven hells.

"I don't understand what you're getting at," Asher murmured, as confused as the moment fae had dragged him out to the woods. "Honestly, Landi, I'm not trying to argue. I just—"

"Don't lie to me," the fae exclaimed. "You know what I thought the moment I saw you guys kiss? That it was a good thing. That you were probably the *one* guy in the entire realm I wouldn't have to worry about." He shook his head with a murderous glare. "My mistake, right?"

Asher stared back at him, in complete bewilderment.

Then it suddenly clicked.

His lips parted and he stepped back with a look of genuine surprise. For a split second, he looked as touched as Evie was herself. Then he shook his head very slowly.

"Nothing happened."

The fae looked at him doubtfully and Asher held up his hands.

"I swear it. You have to know me better than that." He shook his head again, staring back without the hint of a lie. "I wouldn't...I wouldn't let it happen this way."

The men stared at each other another moment then Ellanden nodded sharply, taking a step back. All at once he was very interested in something happening on the ground, or in the sky, or literally any place in the clearing where the vampire didn't happen to be standing.

"Because she deserves a hell of a lot better, you know?" He kicked at the ground, avoiding his friend's gaze, looking decidedly flustered. "And I know it's none of my business. You guys like each other, I get that. I would never have said anything except...why are you smiling?"

"It's nothing," Asher said quickly, trying to control his expression.

"What?"

"You wouldn't like it."

"What?"

"It's just...underneath that horrendous personality...you're actually a good guy."

The princess smacked herself in the forehead as the tension shattered on the spot. There was a burst of laughter, and the boys pushed away from each other with a playful shove.

"No, I'm not," Ellanden said seriously. "I'm not kidding, Asher. Don't ever say that again."

The vampire only grinned, dodging another brotherly swipe.

They were still smiling when they headed out of the clearing. The subject had been swiftly changed to something they were comfortable with (something with no emotional overtones), and things were just picking up speed when the smile faded from the vampire's face.

He watched as the fae stepped out in front of him, saw the black stain of lace-like bruises lacing up the side of his neck. He remembered those as well. He'd made them with his own hands.

"Ellanden—"

The prince glanced over his shoulder, surprised by the sudden change in tone. When he saw the vampire's face, his own smile faded and he continued walking quickly.

"We should get back."

Without another word, he started marching back through the woods...straight towards where the princess was standing. She didn't have time to move. She'd only just made the connection when the ferns suddenly parted and the two of them were standing face to face.

It was difficult to say who looked more surprised. Even more difficult to say who looked more embarrassed. Ellanden froze for a split second before roughly shoving past her, taking care to knock into her shoulder as he went by.

"Shut up."

BY THE TIME THEY GOT back to camp, staggering their arrivals, Cosette and Freya had already cooked and salted most of the rabbit. What little remained was sitting on a bed of leaves, smoking slightly and oozing a deep crimson Evie could only hope had come from the berries and wasn't a grisly reminder of the animal itself. They ate quickly then went to bed—carefully destroying the remains of the fire in case any of the giants had somehow managed to pick up on the trail.

All things considered it was a good shelter, but a tight squeeze. An *awkwardly* tight squeeze, given the circumstances. Acting on the same instinct, both Evie and Asher tried to give each other a wide berth, settling down on opposite sides of the circle. But no matter how many times they shifted position, they kept finding themselves getting pushed back together. The princess had begun to suspect it had something to do with their eternally meddling friends.

"No, you take this spot." Freya rolled over quickly, then patted an open spot of ground with a smile. "That way the two of you can cuddle."

...ex-friends.

The vampire shot her a chilling glare, then gave up the ghost—settling down beside the princess with a quiet sigh. She glanced at him, unwinding her braids.

"Well, this is cozy." Cosette's eyes sparkled as she glanced between them, resting a moment on each one. "Who would have thought?"

This is going to be intolerable.

"And what about you?" the fae continued, glancing up with a grin as Ellanden finished with the fire and joined them inside. "You're okay with this little love-fest?"

The prince flashed them a quick glance, then settled on the opposite side. "Of course," he said easily. "You two should enjoy yourselves while it lasts."

Evie stiffened involuntarily, and Asher's dark eyes shot across the circle. "What does that mean?"

The fae shrugged, settling down beneath his cloak. "Only that, before long, we'll either be dead or back at the castle. If we make it back in one piece, you'll have to try to keep this going under the watchful eyes of Dylan Hale."

He flashed them a sweet smile.

"I don't see that going so well."

In hindsight, that was probably the reason Evie couldn't fall asleep...

Chapter 7

The night was a disaster.

Not because of the cold or the rain, or the cramped quarters, or because those three bites of rabbit had been woefully undercooked. It was a disaster because every time Evie closed her eyes, she saw a far different picture. One that involved a moonlit meadow, a half-naked vampire, and a silent battle to unclasp the buckle on his pants.

A blush stole across her face even as she thought about it, driving her to madness as her eyes shot open and fixed upon the ceiling of their little cave. The others were resting deeply, nothing but the sound of their steady, shallow breaths. Asher appeared to be sleeping as well, but there was no way for her to be sure. After being pressed so shamelessly against each other by the others, they had tried to mitigate the inevitable teasing by facing in opposite directions. Their backs were pressed against one another, but aside from that they were staying completely apart.

Of course he's sleeping. He SHOULD be sleeping. So should you.

That internal voice had grown more and more persistent as the night dragged on, constantly admonishing all those lusty fantasies intent on keeping her awake.

You're on a mission to SAVE THE REALM, remember? Maybe time to stop thinking about the pretty vampire and try to get some sleep?

Easier said than done.

It was like she couldn't escape it. The distracting images paraded shamelessly through her mind.

The little sparks of pain when his fingers knotted in her hair. The feel of his arms tightening around her when his tongue slipped into her mouth. His smooth skin beneath her fingers. His lean body contracting around hers. Then there was always the sight of his teeth sinking into his lower lip as he leaned back on his elbows, gazing up at her with that irresistible grin...

Stop it!

Her body flushed as she pressed her fists into her eyes, as if that could somehow keep the images at bay. How had she never noticed before? How had she been able to tear her eyes away?

Growing up in the castle, the two of them had already shared most every experience one could imagine. They'd attended royal dances with each other, learned to spar with each other, gone swimming with every summer in the enchanted lake. They'd both seen each other wearing far less clothing than they had been just a few hours before, and yet the memory consumed her completely.

Go. To. Sleep.

Her eyes peeked open once again and she decided on a compromise. She *would* go to sleep...just as soon as she checked to see if Asher was sleeping himself.

As quietly as possible, she twisted around beneath her cloak—taking great care not to wake up Cosette, who was sleeping on the other side. The little shelter was so dark, the entire thing might have been a wasted effort. It was so quiet, there was no way anyone could be awake but her.

Then she turned around to find herself staring into a pair of sparkling eyes.

"Can't sleep?"

She pulled in a quick breath, immensely grateful that for once the vampire might not be able to see her blush. He was lying on his side with a hand propped up beneath his head. He was also smiling. The kind of smile that made her think he'd been watching her for a long time.

Her eyes drifted to his lips, then she shook her head quickly. "Nope. What about you?"

He shook his head as well, eyes twinkling in the faint light. "Every time I try, I keep thinking about this girl..."

She bit back a grin, propping herself up the same as him. "Sounds promising. Tell me about her."

He raked back his hair, shaking his head as if it was a bit overwhelming. "Well, she's beautiful. Brave. Opinionated. Decent shot with a bow." He cocked his head thoughtfully, eyes flickering up to the ceiling. "Thinks she's a lot funnier than she is..."

A punishing fist flew towards his face, and he caught it with a grin.

"*Relax*, Everly. You don't know her."

The princess giggled before she could stop herself, stifling the sound in her cloak. "So this mystery girl...why's she keeping you awake?"

He shrugged mischievously, those heated eyes drawing forth another blush. "The thing is, she kind of crawled on top of me—"

Evie clapped a hand over his mouth, glancing quickly at the others. They all appeared to be sleeping. But an eternity of teasing was a heavy price to pay for being wrong about such a thing.

"Would you *shut up*?" she hissed. "It's bad enough they already—"

His lips closed over hers, stealing the last few words right out of her mouth.

For a split second she merely froze, utterly stunned that it was happening. By the time she caught up he was already pulling away, stretching out on his back with a little smile.

"Goodnight, Princess."

She blinked in the darkness, then settled down as well. "...goodnight."

<hr>

BY THE TIME THE SUN rose a few hours later, neither Asher nor Evie felt as though they'd gotten more than a few minutes of rest. Each one sat up slowly, pushing back tangles of messy hair, then wincing as the ceiling was ripped off the little shelter and beams of sunlight came piercing through.

"Good morning!" Ellanden said with a bright smile, tossing the carefully-woven branches into the shrubs. "No point in leaving a trail behind for the giants. Get up—we let you guys sleep long enough!"

The princess and the vampire blinked slowly, wondering if they were really awake.

Already, the little campsite was a thing of the past. The fire had been expertly scattered, the remains of the rabbit carefully hidden away. There was no sign of the girls, but judging by sounds of splashing water and violent oaths they weren't far, just down the slope by the river.

"Must I drag you out of there myself, or are you coming?"

Evie rolled her eyes and pushed to her feet, shaking the pine needles from her cloak before slipping it over her shoulders. There were still a few cooked roots and berries left from the previous night's dinner, but when she reached for them the fae held them up with another obnoxious smile.

"How did everyone sleep?" he asked cheerfully, dangling the food out of reach. "Hopefully you got some more rest than my friend Asher. Poor guy was tossing and turning all night."

The vampire ran his tongue over his teeth, fighting the urge to bare his fangs.

Evie went straight for open violence, striking the fae with a tree branch before taking the roots and berries for herself. "I'm so glad you're enjoying all this."

He flashed a wicked grin, shaking the leaves from his hair. "Well at least one of us should be enjoying themselves. And seeing as the two of you have come up against a bit of a wall—"

"Flasks are filled. Clothes are clean." Cosette nodded a quick greeting to the others as she and Freya returned from the woods. "Morning, guys. Have any intimate late-night discussions?"

The couple froze at the same time, while Ellanden shot her a sour look.

"I was just getting to that."

"No time," his cousin replied sweetly, cocking her head towards the trees. "We've got to get moving if we want to find a village and stock up on supplies before nightfall. We may have left the giants behind, but there's still plenty more that can kill us in this forest. I, for one, want a weapon."

The playful mood faded slightly as each of the friends recognized their plight.

Being lost in the middle of the woods with no supplies and no weapons was one of the fastest ways imaginable to get yourself killed. Granted, the gang had a few things on their side. The witch, for one. The vampire, for another. Not to mention the fact that each of the others knew at least fifty ways to kill a man with their bare hands.

But those kinds of skills didn't mean much against a long-range weapon. A pair of bandits with a bow could do just as much damage without taking nearly so much of a risk. They needed to arm up. This new world was nothing to be taken lightly.

"And how do you suggest we buy these weapons?" Ellanden asked innocently, taking his place in the front as they eased back onto the mountain trail. "Should we barter with the girls?"

A punishing volley of sparks hit the back of his head, while Asher simply rolled his eyes.

"Not your famous horse-thief idea again."

"I'm telling you, it's the only way," the fae insisted. "And you wouldn't have to do any of the work if it offends your delicate sensibilities. I'm more than happy to take care of it myself."

Asher nodded wisely, keeping his eyes on the trail.

"Because if there's one thing we vampires are known for, it's our delicate sensibilities..."

For the next few hours, the friends continued walking along the alpine trail. The air was bitter cold, considering winter had passed them, but as they made their way slowly out of mountains the world began to thaw. Little flowers began peeking through the foliage. Birds darted through the canopy above them, lifting their voices on the breeze. The rocky night was forgotten and the gang was actually starting to enjoy themselves, when the trail spilled suddenly onto a well-paved road.

The three friends jumped down immediately. The witch and the fae instinctively held back.

"Does the trail continue on the other side?" Cosette called quietly, glancing up and down the road. "Maybe there's another path we could follow—"

"Yes, *or* we could take the conveniently-located road," Evie interrupted, gesturing theatrically around her. "The quickest way to find a village is by staying right on here."

Cosette pursed her lips, while Freya shook her head.

"We can't travel on the main road. It isn't safe."

Asher scoffed impatiently, while Ellanden smiled like she'd said something adorable.

"While I admire the caution, between the five of us—"

"The *five* of us are the problem," the witch interrupted shortly. "A lot's changed since you guys dozed off in that wizard's cave. Fae are coveted. Vampires are not a welcome sight. You guys think you're so formidable. That's great. But you're also a target."

The prince's smile faded ever so slightly as the vampire glanced carefully up the road.

"Well, what about the two of us?" Evie suggested, nodding at the witch. "We could go on ahead and see if there was—"

"*Absolutely* not," the men said together.

"The world might be different," Ellanden murmured, "but some things will never change."

The princess' eyes flashed as she placed her hands on her hips.

"What's that supposed to mean? I'm not a vampire. I'm not a fae—"

"No, but you're a beautiful woman." Asher gave her with a little wink. "You're in the most danger of all."

Ellanden threw up his hands impatiently. "So what does that mean? You expect us to make it all the way to the sea by taking nothing but remote mountain trails? I'm all for caution, but we really don't have that kind of time..."

He trailed off mid-sentence, lifting his eyes to the road. The vampire was already staring, brow creased with a slight frown. After a moment, they threw each other a quick glance.

"A few men and a wagon. Couldn't be more than ten."

The vampire nodded, lifting his chin as if sniffing the breeze.

"Fewer than that. And there's something else...fish?"

"Perhaps they're merchants," Cosette inserted. "Few are bold enough to travel, what with the lack of royal enforcement, but others have no choice."

"Even merchants come heavily armed," Freya muttered, folding her arms across her chest.

Asher listened another moment, then shook his head slowly. "I don't think they're merchants. I could have sworn—"

But what he was about to say, the others would never know. Because at that very moment, a little caravan of people made their way around the bend in the road.

The fae let down their hair quickly in some useless attempt to hide what they were, while the vampire flipped up the hood of his cloak. Wise precautions, but if they were fearing some kind of ambush they needn't have worried. The men coming towards them looked as surprised to see them as they were to have stumbled upon the caravan themselves.

"Good morning!" the one in the front called preemptively, waving a cautious hand. The roads were no longer what they used to be. Even when travelling with a decent-sized force, one had to be careful. "And what brings you fellow travelers so far on the northern road?"

His face relaxed ever so slightly when he saw they were young. He relaxed even more when he saw they were unarmed. Then it sharpened with a smile as he started making plans.

Ellanden approached warily, flashing a polite smile himself. "Just doing a little scouting before returning to the rest of our group." His eyes flickered swiftly over the horses. "We heard there might be a village nearby."

The man glanced back the way he'd come. "Just five miles or so, though I wouldn't exactly call it a village." He stared a second longer than was warranted, studying the young man with the hint of a frown. "You from around these parts?"

Ellanden nodded casually, checking for weapons at the same time. "Not far."

"Well, don't let us delay you," Freya inserted with a tight smile. "We have miles to go and it's already mid-day…"

She tried to take a step forward, but the man didn't move. A faint grin lit his face as he looked her up and down, eyes flashing over the rest of the gang.

"You're a strange group," he murmured, almost to himself. There was a quick double-take when he got to Asher—who quickly glanced away. "You going to the village to trade?"

"Perhaps," Ellanden said bracingly, already wishing they'd taken the girls' advice and gotten the hell off the main road. "Like I said, we're only scouting. It depends on the rest of our group."

The man nodded slowly, fighting back a smile. "Your group…of course." Instead of stepping aside to let them through he leaned casually against the side of the wagon, smiling as five other men stood loosely by his side. "Though, if you are meaning to trade, I'm sure we could provide whatever you might be looking for."

His gaze felt on the three girls.

"For a price, of course."

Evie stiffened dramatically, while the vampire hissed quietly by her side.

At that point, Ellanden decided to embrace his original plan.

"Well, I hardly have the authority to allow something like that," he said sweetly, stepping amongst their ranks under the guise of examining the horses. "But it isn't out of the question."

When we get to this mysterious village...I'm officially murdering the fae.

"If you like, I'd be happy to relay your offer to the others," he continued. "They should be along shortly. And I know there were things they were hoping to acquire."

His fingers trailed lightly down the harness, slipping out the nearest hook. It was so casually done, Evie wouldn't have noticed it herself if she hadn't been looking. One down, three more to go.

"Ah yes?" the man said conversationally, casting a backwards glance at his men. "And what are those? You'll find we have quite the selection."

Another hook down. Then another after that.

You've got it—just one more. Then we'll we leave this place in the dust.

"Just the usual," Ellanden answered casually, running his hand along a horse's neck. "Rope and a canteen, my friends were hoping for a bow—"

He looked down suddenly, stiffening in surprise. His hand froze above the final loop in the harness before he backed away swiftly, abandoning the enterprise altogether.

Evie stared in astonishment at the back of his head.

Come on! You're backing out now?

Without a second thought, she stepped forward to replace him—bypassing the vampire's restraining hand and flashing the man in charge a charming smile.

"So now you know everything about us, what about you? Where are you headed?"

Ellanden shook his head discreetly, but she ignored him—running her hand along the horse's neck just as he'd done himself. Just a few more inches, then she'd free the final loop.

"There's no clear destination," the man answered, watching the princess with a predatory smile. "We tend to go wherever opportunity takes us."

Her fingers slid smoothly down the leather, coming to rest on the metal circle.

"That's *fascinating*," Ellanden said sharply, a silent warning in his eyes. "But Freya's right, we really should be leaving—"

"What's the hurry?" the man interrupted with a twinkling smile. "It looks like your friend here is just getting comfortable, and it isn't often we get to see such a pretty face." His arms folded as he looked her up and down. "I can only imagine the talents she's picked up on the road..."

Evie's eyes flashed as she unclasped the final circle. "You have no idea—"

A splash of water hit the back of her neck.

...what the hell?

In what felt like slow motion she looked over her shoulder, watching as the 'horse' she'd been freeing shook free of the harness, lifting a pair of huge leathery wings. The scent of rotting kelp swept over the caravan as she tripped a step backwards, staring in open-mouthed surprise.

"Kelpies," the man said dryly. "I wouldn't get too close."

Holy crap!

The princess swallowed hard, rooted to the spot.

"Hard to ride," he continued casually, pulling a large knife from his belt. "Even harder to steal, though I have to admit I'm impressed you were brave enough to try. Your friend over there thought better of it. Probably saved his own life in the process."

Ellanden's eyes snapped shut for a split second before he yanked the princess back.

The others were already clustered nervously around them, hyper-aware of the fact that each of the men standing in front of them was heavily armed. And there were more in the wagon.

"I'm afraid there's been a misunderstanding," the fae murmured respectfully, angling Evie safely behind him. "We're sorry to have wasted your time—"

"What are you talking about?" The man grabbed the harness and ripped it loose, freeing the pack of kelpies with a wicked smile. "The fun's just getting started..."

Chapter 8

The thing about fighting a kelpie was that you never knew exactly what you were going to get. They could take the form of a mighty stallion, a beautiful woman, or even sometimes a beautiful man. No matter the appearance, the goal was always the same: to drag even the most skilled warrior to the nearest source of water before devouring them in the depths.

That was the best-case scenario. Sometimes they played with you a little first.

The first time Evie had seen one she'd been about eight years old, riding in the woods with her father. They'd stopped beside a pond to give their horses a drink, only to find a small herd of similar-looking animals lingering curiously on the other side.

"Look, Daddy!" she'd cried in delight. "Ponies!"

That's when her father—her brave, fearless father—leapt back onto his horse and headed straight back the way they'd come, keeping a protective hand on his daughter the entire time.

There were days when you had to pick your battles.

This was one of those days.

"RUN!"

No sooner had the first creature unfurled its mighty wings than a hand grabbed Evie by the back of the cloak and yanked her out of reach. The men were shouting. The kelpies were baying. A volley of sparks fired into the air. Then a moment later, the friends were in full retreat.

Kelpies! Evie threw a look over her shoulder. *I can't believe they're bloody kelpies!*

As a single unit, the gang outpaced the people chasing them and streaked back up the road…only to realize that the caravan was a unit of its own. And they'd only met the first half.

"What the …?" Ellanden panted.

An arrow whizzed past Evie's head, catching in her long hair as yet another wagon appeared at the other end of the road, fencing them in. They screeched to a stop, staring in dismay. While this one didn't appear to be pulled by anything more interesting than a pair of donkeys, that spilt second break in momentum had given the enemy all the time they needed to catch up.

The kelpies were upon them a moment later. The men were close behind.

"*Shit!*"

The princess would never know who had shouted, because just a split second later the two caravans reunited, trapping them together in the middle of the road.

That's when the fighting got dirty.

It was hard not to panic when assaulted by a herd of demonic horses, and these seemed more badly-tempered than most. With expert precision they attacked the five teenagers at strategic angles, fracturing their attempts to stay together and driving them further apart.

Cosette was struck across the face with the back of a dagger. Ellanden flew forward to help, and was thrown clear across the road. Every time the friends tried to focus on the monstrous beasts attacking them, the men would take advantage of their distraction and launch coordinated attacks of their own. Every time they fended off the men, the kelpies would swoop in for the kill.

"Evie!"

The princess whirled around just as a pair of razor-sharp hooves pawed the air above her, coming down with deadly force where she'd been standing a moment before. The ground shook and she stumbled back, straight into the arms of the man she'd been chatting with before.

"So how about it, sweetheart…?" He clasped his arms around her waist, whispering in her ear. "Care to show me some of those talents?"

She flung her head backward, hitting him right in the nose. "I'd *love* to!"

As the battle raged on around her she turned to face him head-on, glaring with the strength of a nova as they squared off in the middle of the road. Even twice her age, even twice her size, he didn't really stand a chance. The princess might have been outnumbered and unarmed, but she'd been trained by the best the realm had to offer. Just a moment later, he was bleeding on the ground.

"If only we had more time." She dodged a knife-attack from one of the others, hurling it with precision aim right in the center of his stomach. "There's so much more for you to see."

She would have done more. The adrenaline was surging, the battle was raging, and for the first time in longer than she cared to remember she found herself armed with a blade. But no sooner had she lifted it into the air than it was kicked straight out of her hand.

"Son of a harpy!" she cursed, whirling around to find herself face to face with a gigantic black stallion. Her eyes widened slightly as she took a step back. "I mean...my mistake."

There was a split second pause then, before her very eyes, the stallion vanished—melting and re-shifting into something that vaguely resembled a man. He stood just as tall as the horse and smiled at her invitingly, green eyes flashing as he held out a hand.

"Don't struggle, child. It will only be harder if you do."

Scattered about the road, the friends were finding themselves in a similar position. Most of the men had been dispatched, or at least knocked temporarily out of the fighting, but it was hard enough dealing with just one kelpie and the herd had them surrounded.

Most had remained horses. But as Evie cast a quick look over her shoulder, the one standing beside Asher shimmered suddenly. A beautiful naked woman appeared in its place.

"A vampire," she murmured, reaching out to touch his hair. "It's been a long time since I've had a vampire. Most of your kind stay well away from these parts."

He froze where he stood, momentarily stunned.

"Come with me, pretty vampire," she purred. "Come down to the river. No one will harm you. You have my word."

He took a bracing step back amidst the chaos, fangs sinking into his lip. But before he could make up his mind how best to attack, her hand flashed out and closed around his wrist.

From a distance, it looked like the two were merely standing there. Then the princess saw the muscles straining in the vampire's arm. A look of panic flashed across his face when nothing happened. When he tried jerking back again, half the bones snapped in his wrist.

He let out a quiet gasp. The kelpie tilted her head with a smile.

"ASHER!"

Evie let out a scream as the demonic woman pulled him right off his feet—whipping around in the same instant and dragging him down the hill. She didn't have to hear the river to know there was water nearby. And there wasn't a doubt in her mind that the second Asher slipped under those murky waves...he wasn't coming out.

Only a few seconds had passed, but those seconds changed everything.

In a daze she turned back to her own monster, glancing down at his outstretched hand. If they touched you, it was over. That much was clear. Asher was already gone, and judging by the screams and struggles she was hearing around her the others weren't far behind.

Cosette was holding two of them off, but at this point it was clear she was simply trying to escape. Freya had been knocked unconscious the second it became clear she could throw fire. And while Ellanden had managed to slay one of the beasts, the others had rallied around him in a vengeful rage—pawing the ground in fury, screaming how they were going to punish such a crime.

No one had seen the vampire disappear. No one had much time left themselves.

Evie lifted her eyes to the kelpie, staring in silence as her body went suddenly calm. Strands of black, brackish hair were dripping down the sides of his neck. His green eyes glowed hypnotically as they swept over her, reaching a bit farther with his outstretched hand.

"Come, now," he soothed. "We'll go down together—"

But the princess was no longer there. A wolf had sprung up in her place.

You want to go down together?

There was quiet gasp as the man dropped his hand, stumbling back towards the others.

The way most people weren't fond of snakes, most kelpies had an instinctual aversion to snarling dogs. Especially when those dogs came with a set of razor-sharp, fang-like teeth.

It wasn't much of a fight. The princess didn't have time for much of a fight. Careful not to let the beast lay a hand on her body, she vaulted up into the air—slashing out at his exposed neck in the same instant. There was a screeching howl as he fell to his knees, twitching and writhing as the man vanished and a dying horse appeared in his place. The sight was enough to draw the shocked eyes of the others, but before they could launch a counter-attack the wolf was upon them as well.

Her friends dropped to the ground, ducking out of the way as she leapt from one creature to another. Biting and scratching as she went. Savaging whatever bit of flesh she could as giant arches of blood flew into the sky. The screams that followed became less and less human. After only a few seconds, there was nothing human about them at all.

That's right...run.

There was pandemonium as the herd scattered, flying in every direction as the wolf leapt after them, continuing its vicious assault. She dodged the frantic kicks and easily outpaced them, slashing at their exposed legs and driving them away from her friends.

It could have gone on forever. In a bloodshot haze the princess saw only moving targets, with not much room for any other rational thought.

Then Ellanden let out a sudden shout. "Where's Asher!"

The princess stopped dead in her tracks. With a sudden chill she looked over her shoulder, heightened senses zeroing in as she heard the sound of a distant splash.

In a streak of crimson fur, she was gone.

IN HINDSIGHT IT MUST have taken only a few seconds for a wolf to reach the base of the mountain, but Evie would swear it felt much longer. She lived and died with each passing moment, springing through the underbrush with her own frantic breaths ringing in her ears.

There had been splashing once, but there wasn't any longer. Everything was quiet now.

She could only imagine what that might mean.

With a final burst of speed she leapt over a fallen tree and cleared the last of the ferns, only to come screeching to a stop on the shore of a river. There was no sign of them. The vampire and the kelpie had simply disappeared. Yet there was a violent progression of tracks leading down to the water. Every so often, those tracks were darkened with a splash of blood.

The princess didn't think. She simply leapt into the water.

It might have been harder to think clearly as a wolf, but it was easier to run and it was easier to fight. It was easier to swim as well. With effortless speed she cut through the choppy waves, paddling out to the very center before taking a deep breath and plunging down into the depths.

It was like stepping into a dream.

At once, the chaos of the world above vanished and things went strangely still. The picture around her shimmered, then cleared. The mist of bubbles faded, and for a brief crystalline moment she was able to see everything in perfect detail.

...starting with the two people standing on the riverbed.

It was utterly bizarre—as if they were merely having a conversation. A beautiful girl and a beautiful boy, chatting together at the bottom of an alpine river. Only, if one looked closer, it was clear that she was actually keeping him there. That instead of devouring him immediately, as was the eventual goal, she'd decided to play with him a little—allowing him to drown instead.

Ash!

For a split second Evie watched in horror, floating twenty feet above them.

His kind might have been gifted with speed and strength, but they had no special talent when it came to avoiding asphyxiation. And the lack of oxygen was already starting to show.

That deadly grace had vanished. His movements were awkward and slow. His already-pale skin looked almost translucent, reflecting the blue waves, and after each faltering attempt to free himself he stilled even more dramatically, like he was nothing more than a lovely reanimated corpse.

"I'm sorry to do it this way..."

Those dark eyes widened as the kelpie pressed a sudden kiss to his lips, raking her claws down his cheeks. She lingered a moment, then pulled back with a wicked smile.

"...but I think you'll appreciate the irony of what happens next."

His head jerked back a second later as the monster sank her teeth into his skin. There was a silent scream, a cloud of swirling crimson as he thrashed frantically, trying to dislodge her from his neck. But there was no fighting such a thing. It was a simple move, designed to kill.

One that the vampire had used countless times himself. But he'd never known how it felt until that very moment.

Of course, kelpies weren't interested in drinking blood. This one had come to feed.

There was an abrupt burrowing motion as the last of the charade fell away and the creature tore away a chunk of flesh. This time, she heard the scream. Asher's eyes flashed bright with pain before dimming just as suddenly. His pale hands relaxed abruptly and drifted up into her hair.

From that point on, his memory failed him.

He scarcely even saw when the giant wolf appeared between them, didn't notice when it bit the kelpie in half with a single jerk of its head. The most he could do was keep his eyes open as it batted the body away and swam towards him, staring in surreal wonder at the giant wolf.

At this point, there was no way to tell what he was thinking. Had he made the connection that the predator was actually his girlfriend? Did he simply think the stars had aligned against him, and one way or another he was to be devoured on a forgotten riverbed?

It was anyone's guess.

But he lifted his arms obediently when the princess nudged her head against him, letting them circle around her neck. Letting himself be lifted up through the waves as they left the nightmare behind them, heading back towards the light...

Chapter 9

"ASHER!" Evie screamed his name the second their heads broke the surface. The transition, which had been so difficult before, happened seamlessly this time as the fur vanished from her body. Leaving behind a slender, naked girl with huge, terrified eyes.

"ASH!"

There was no response. His body floated lifelessly beside her as his head fell limp on her shoulder. Her first instinct was to simply shake him out of it, but she found herself too frightened to even look. If the crimson pool around them was any indication, the vampire wasn't in good shape.

A sound of distant footsteps echoed through the trees as she dragged his body onto the shore. The others had heard the call and were coming as fast as they could, but no matter how soon they reached the river the princess didn't see what they'd be able to do.

She let out a silent gasp, looking down at him for the first time. It wasn't the color of his skin, or the ghastly bruises, or the fact that his beautiful eyes were closed. It was his neck.

...what was left of it.

Seven hells.

There was so much missing, she didn't see how it had stayed attached. There was so much missing, there was hardly any blood. It was as if the fight was already over, and his body had reached the end. Her hands came up in a sort of prayer as her eyes spilled over with tears.

"Please...please don't be dead."

The rest of the friends burst onto the riverbank a moment later, taking only a second to orient themselves before freezing with matching expressions of shock. Cosette's hands flew over her mouth as Freya caught her in a strategic embrace, angling her away from the sight. Ellanden's lips parted in breathless horror before his handsome face went suddenly still.

"Is he—" He took a faltering step towards them, unable to summon the words. "Is he—"

The vampire's fingers twitched, and the clearing came back to life.

"Was that him?!" Cosette trilled, whirling back around. "Did he just move?!"

Ellanden dove towards them, sending up a spray of pebbles as he knelt beside Evie. He didn't seem to notice she was naked. She didn't seem to notice he was dripping blood.

"The kelpie pulled him under," she gasped, feeling like her chest was ripping in two. "I tried to get there in time, but—"

"He's still alive," Ellanden interrupted, carefully putting the vampire's head in his lap.

A gentle finger pressed the inside of his wrist, searching for a pulse. Another rested lightly on his parted lips, searching for a breath. But there was none to be found.

A look of sheer panic swept over him before his eyes flashed to the princess.

"You can heal him."

I can...what?

A hushed silence fell between them.

The thought hadn't even occurred to her. Vampires were the ones who possessed magical healing powers, not shifters. But when the wounded person happened to *be* a vampire?

"Of course," she gasped, holding out a hand. "Give me your blade."

Cosette's eyes widened as she took a step closer.

"You're...you're giving him your blood? You're making a bond?"

"I'm *healing* him," Evie corrected quickly, slashing the inside of her wrist.

"He'll die otherwise," Ellanden murmured, taking back the knife and wiping it distractedly on the leg of his pants. "And besides, they're already bonded."

The fae's mouth fell open, and Freya stared between them in surprise.

"When did—"

But there was no time for explanations. A moment later, and with very little finesse, Evie pressed her bleeding skin over Asher's mouth. Trembling all the while, waiting for the inevitable bite, watching with breathless anticipation for the slightest hint of change.

...but nothing happened.

"Why isn't it working?" she said urgently, giving her wrist an unnecessary shake. Seconds were ticking past, seconds they didn't have to waste. "Landi, he isn't—"

The fae grabbed her wrist, squeezing it slightly as he opened Asher's mouth wider with the other hand. Together, the two of them leaned over and watched the blood trickle slowly down his throat. Waiting on pins and needles, unable to pull in a full breath.

Come on, Asher. Open those eyes.

A full minute passed. Then another minute after that.

There wasn't a sound on the riverbank. The friends had never been so still. Then a lone bird started singing somewhere above them. A quiet, plaintive song that sounded like the end.

"This isn't happening," Evie whispered, shaking from head to toe. "Tell me this isn't real."

There was a flash of silver as Ellanden reopened the wound on her wrist, fingers trembling slightly as he pressed the blood firmly against his friend's mouth.

"He's going to make it," he murmured, willing it to be true. "He *has* to make it."

But he isn't going to make it! He's already gone!

The princess let out a breathless sob, turning her face to the sky as the fae continued to hold out her arm. Hysterical tears slid down her cheeks as the world flickered in panic.

"I don't believe it!" she gasped, starting to hyperventilate. "We were too late!" Another sob ripped through her, even more devastating than the last. "We were just too—"

But at that moment everything changed.

Because at that moment the vampire opened his eyes.

"...Asher?"

Evie's head whipped back around at the sound of Ellanden's voice, staring down shock. It wasn't immediately clear whether the vampire could hear him. Those dark eyes were simply travelling between the two, resting a moment on each face. Then they found the blood.

Shit!

The princess let out an involuntary cry as a pair of fangs tore into her, ripping clean through one vein before digging into another. A vise-like pressure was soon to follow—so unrelenting and intense it brought a quiet whimper to her lips.

"Ash," the fae tempered quickly, pressing him down with a firm hand, "it's okay. She isn't going anywhere, just—"

The vampire struck him across the face, grabbing Evie's arm in both hands as he half-lifted off the ground. His world was sharpening rapidly, while hers was starting to dim. He was vaguely aware of a tingling in his neck, but he didn't know what it meant.

All that mattered was the blood. And getting more of it.

"*Asher!*" Ellanden shouted, whipping out the same trusted blade. Without a second's pause he pressed it to the vampire's chest, forcing him back down again. "That's *enough*!"

If anything, the pressure increased—bringing with it a merciful sense of relief as a strange numbing sensation started travelling up the princess' arm. Her eyes fluttered without permission as the pebbly shore tilted suddenly to the side. Another few seconds and she would have blacked out entirely, if the fangs hadn't suddenly vanished, replaced with a set of supportive arms.

"Evie!"

This time, it wasn't Ellanden who was shouting, it was Asher himself. He'd pushed straight past the prince's blade to catch her before she could fall—ignoring his own wounds entirely as he cradled her gently in his arms. A cloak was produced from nowhere, draped lightly over her skin.

When she finally managed to open her eyes, he looked the same as he always did. Granted, a bit paler and wetter, and bloodier than he'd been before.

"Are you all right?" he asked breathlessly, trailing a finger down the side of her face. "I'm so sorry, Everly. I wasn't able to stop—"

Her head fell back against him as her lips curved up in a drowsy smile "I knew it," she murmured, drifting off to sleep. "They weren't ponies after all..."

CONSIDERING HOW MUCH blood she'd lost, the princess didn't sleep long. She was already coming out of it by the time the friends carried her away from the riverbank and into the trees. If anything, the one having a tough time shaking what had happened was Asher.

Not only was he jumping at the slightest noise, but one hand kept drifting to his neck. Like he was subconsciously checking to make sure it was still there.

"Do you think this is good?" he asked the others, one foot bouncing up and down as his jittery hands ran through his hair. "Do you think we really lost them? Because if you think there's a chance they could still find us, we could walk a little farther. I wouldn't mind walking farther."

The girls shared a quick look, while Ellanden set the princess down with an amused grin. In spite of the vampire's strong insistence to carry her, the fae had elected to do it himself. Mostly because the girl was still bleeding and he didn't want the smell of it under the vampire's nose. There was also a chance that Asher could have dropped her in his present state.

"We're fine here," he said for the tenth time. "You weren't there for Evie's little wolf-attack, but I guarantee those kelpies remember. We won't be seeing them any time soon."

The vampire glanced twice between them then nodded quickly, settling down on the grass.

It was an abruptly awkward moment. The shock at the riverside and the subsequent journey through the forest had successfully dampened whatever inevitable conversations might be brewing. But now that the gang had stopped, all those questions floated right back to the surface.

It didn't help matters when the princess opened her eyes.

"Hey," Asher said immediately, leaning past Ellanden to take her hands, "you're awake! It hasn't been long. Don't worry about it having been long. A little less than an hour, really. But the others think we're safe. I think we're safe, too. Of course, if you don't think we're safe, then I'd be happy to keep walking. I could even carry you this time. Ellanden didn't let me do that before."

Evie lifted her eyebrows slowly, turning to the prince.

"He's been like this since the river," Ellanden murmured with a touch of amusement. "I'm guessing it has something to do with being full of your blood."

That would make sense.

The night before the legendary Battle of the Dunes, their parents had apparently done the same thing—sealing themselves into an eternal union, bonded forever with immortal blood.

In the years that followed, there was occasionally a need to refresh such ties.

Never was such a thing done by choice. But, given the often volatile temperament of the monarchs in question, along with their unfortunate tendency to get into trouble, they sometimes found themselves in desperate need of healing.

Nothing could be scarier in the moment.

Nothing could be funnier in the moments immediately to come.

Twinning, as her Aunt Tanya liked to call it, was perhaps the only light-hearted aspect of having formed a bond. For however long a time after, the person who consumed the blood would take on trademark characteristics of the first. It resulted in a mirrored personality. Horrifically embarrassing to the person being mimicked. Endlessly entertaining for those who got to watch.

"I'm not..." Asher trailed off indignantly, staring between them. "This isn't..." He scowled at their matching expressions, folding his arms tight across his chest. "You have no idea what you're talking about. Maybe *you're* the ones who have lost perspective. Did you ever think of that?"

Evie and Ellanden shared a quick look.

"I rest my case."

The princess fought back a grin as the vampire scowled even harder, shooting petulant glances at the fae. She was just thinking of ways to start messing with him, when Cosette knelt suddenly on her other side, checking the bloody bandage tied around her wrist.

"Of course, it wouldn't be the first time he's tasted your blood," she said lightly, dark eyes jumping between each one. "Apparently, it's happened before. *Apparently*, the two of you bonded."

The three friends froze suddenly, not knowing what to say. Sometimes it was easy to slip back into their old dynamic—a trio of kindred spirits, no time for anyone else. Sometimes it was easy to forget that Cosette had earned her place among them, that she and Freya were the same age.

Evie grimaced apologetically. "There may be some things we've forgotten to say..."

Freya plopped down beside them—either legitimately oblivious, or deliberately ignoring the tension. Her eyes lit up with curiosity as they rested upon the princess and the vampire in turn.

"So do you guys feel different now?" she asked excitedly, unconcerned by the intimate nature of such a question. "Is that why you started dating?"

Ellanden glanced up sharply at the word *dating*, but the new couple averted their eyes with an identical blush. It wasn't like they hadn't thought about it. It wasn't like they hadn't asked themselves the same question before. But between the fact that it was a one-sided bond and Asher's romantic declaration that he'd cared for her long before tasting her blood, they'd put the subject to rest.

...at least for the time being.

"Of course not," Asher said quietly, still avoiding everyone's eyes. "These things don't work like that, Freya. And the bond was strictly unintentional."

Unintentional, maybe.

But it had happened twice now. And the second time had saved his life.

"Does it get stronger the more times it happens?" the witch continued curiously, wide eyes taking up almost half her face. "Does it give you guys an edge in a fight? Because if it does, then at this point we should probably all try it—"

"*No!*" The three friends shouted at the same time.

"It's not something to be taken lightly," Ellanden replied, recovering his composure. "And it's not something you enter into unless there's no other choice."

"It also doesn't strengthen the more times you do it," Evie added. "A bond is a bond. The only way to increase it is to share blood the other way. And that...has its own set of complications."

Massive understatement.

Those 'complications' were the reason her father had once tried to stab Uncle Aidan. Those same 'complications' were the reason her brave Uncle Kailas was secretly afraid of bears.

"So how did you know they were kelpies?"

The princess tuned back in with a look of surprise as Freya jumped manically from one subject to the next. She was looking at the fae now, waiting expectantly for an answer.

"...sorry?"

"The horses," she repeated. "How did you know they were kelpies? You stopped yourself a second before freeing them. Then I saw you trying to wave Evie back."

Thank you SO MUCH for reminding him...

"Oh, right." He leaned back in the grass, propped up on his elbows. "Their hooves," he answered, face tightening as he remembered. "Their hooves were backwards."

Sure enough, that memory triggered something else.

"And you're right," he continued, twisting around to give Evie a chilling glare. "I *did* try to wave her back. I guess someone was feeling a little too sure of herself."

"Oh come on," she shot back caustically, waving her bandage in the air. "You really don't think I've paid for that by now?"

"The vampire had his turn," the fae answered with a wicked grin. "Now I think it's time for the rest of us. Cosette, hand me that dagger. Time for a little lesson in paying attention—"

But the fae wasn't the only one having adrenaline-fueled flashbacks. The second Freya had said the word 'kelpies', the vampire had gone very still. His eyes fixed upon Ellanden, and a second before he could take the knife he appeared right in front of him, blowing back the fae's white hair.

"I'm sorry."

Ellanden stared back in shock, startled by the sudden proximity.

"What are you talking about? Sorry for what?"

The vampire merely shook his head, a living portrait of shame.

"I never knew..." he began, then trailed into silence. "Before today, I never..."

The friends shared a quick look, absolutely baffled. The fae looked borderline worried, like there might be something wrong with Asher's head. On instinct, he grabbed the princess' wrist and thrust it back towards the vampire's mouth.

"Have another drink," he offered. "You're clearly unwell."

Evie yanked her arm back with a scowl as Asher pushed to his feet—waiting until the fae took the hint and stood up as well. One was wary. The other was a picture of remorse.

"I couldn't move," he said softly. "The fight was over, I thought I was going to die. Then when she bit into me..." His eyes tightened as his head bowed in shame. "Ellanden, I'm *so* sorry to have done that to you."

A heavy silence fell over the clearing.

Ellanden was speechless. Even Freya found herself at a loss for words. Cosette froze in a moment of total shock, then flashed a glare at the princess.

Yeah, there might be a few more things we didn't say...

There had been many apologies since that day in the tunnel. Many broken promises and sudden punches thrown without a hint of regret. But, for whatever reason, this one felt different.

This time, Ellanden didn't say it was all right. It wasn't all right. But it also wasn't the vampire's fault. Just like the lingering rage, the lingering mistrust, and the lingering stab of fear whenever he lay down beside his best friend and closed his eyes wasn't any fault of his own.

"I know."

It was the best they were going to get.

And maybe, one day, it would be enough.

"So...what are we going to do now?"

The gang turned to Freya with the same incredulous expression. Cosette kicked her for good measure. "You *really* don't know when to shut up, do you?"

"What?" the witch exclaimed, throwing up her hands. "I thought they were finished."

The others rolled their eyes in exasperation, but Ellanden flashed her a quick grin.

"No, that's all right. It's a good question."

Now that the caravans were demolished and their pack of avenging kelpies was on the run, it seemed like a good idea to move as fast as they could in the opposite direction. Then again, they still needed supplies. Most importantly, weapons. Perhaps there was a different option to choose.

"You think it's too risky going to this village?" Evie asked quietly, flashing the rest of them a look. "They knew it's where we were headed. But after all that, they have to think—"

"—they have to think there's *no way* we'd possibly follow through," Ellanden finished.

Asher pursed his lips with a thoughtful frown. "They have to think that because no one in their right mind *would* follow through."

Evie shot him a sideways glance. "That doesn't sound like me."

"No," Ellanden agreed, "it's way too cynical."

They waited a moment, until the vampire rolled his eyes.

"What can I say? I'm feeling more and more like myself."

The others chuckled quietly, then stared in thoughtful silence at the trees.

There had been too many close calls the last few weeks to ignore. First the leopards, then the giants, then the herd of murderous river-monsters intent on eating them alive. That wasn't even to mention their run-in with a vengeful gang of shifters, or the sorcerer who'd come before.

Their streak of bad luck had gone on long enough.

Something was bound to break in their favor.

"I say we go to the village," Cosette said suddenly, pushing to her feet. "Freya and I didn't make it this far by keeping to the shadows. If we need supplies for our journey to the Dunes, then we're going to have to start somewhere. No point in hiding out, hoping the problem goes away."

Ellanden got to his feet beside her, staring down with a hint of pride. "Sometimes I wonder what happened to the little girl from the castle," he teased. "The one who was frightened of spiders and ran around with flowers in her hair."

Cosette flashed a faint grin before spinning a dagger into her pack. "Oh, she's still around. She's just not afraid of spiders anymore."

Chapter 10

The friends may have decided to continue their journey to the village, but they no longer had any intention of travelling by the main road. The kelpie attack had pushed them a ways off course, but they were still only a few miles away and reached it just as the sun set through the trees.

For once, Evie was the first to have seen it. Still brimming with the success of her wolf-attack, she'd insisted upon taking the fae's usual place at the lead. (There was also the fact that beneath her emerald cloak, she was no longer wearing any clothes.)

"Landi," she called over her shoulder, frowning at the lights twinkling below, "where exactly did you say the alpine path would lead us?"

"Just to the middle country," he replied with a shrug. "A bunch of hamlets and villages. We should be able to make our way through fairly quickly before securing passage on a ship."

The princess frowned, then glanced back at Cosette for confirmation. The younger fae just shook her head. "Don't ask me. I've never been out this far. Everything past the Pengrass Forest is beyond royal jurisdiction. What's *left* of royal jurisdiction," she amended.

"What's the matter?" Asher asked quietly, joining the princess at the top of the bluff. "What do you see?"

She paused before answering, gazing into the valley below. "I'm not exactly sure."

Despite the varied locations, most of the villages in the five kingdoms looked generally the same. There was a handful of taverns, a blacksmith, a butcher, a laundress and, if you were very lucky, some kind of healer or apothecary where you could stock up before going on your way.

This...wasn't like that.

It was as if someone had built one village, then stacked ten more on top of it. Then scattered ten more around that. Then added an arena, a list, a live shooting range, and enough well-stocked bars that the princess could hear a chorus of drunken shouting from all the way in the trees.

The only thing missing was the healer. Although there was a large field of freshly turned dirt at the other edge of the encampment, as if anyone who lost step was thrown into a massive grave.

"Well, that looks lovely," Freya said with a bright smile. "Shall we head down?"

The others stared at her a moment before returning their attention to the camp. Even as they were watching, a door burst open on one of the taverns and a trio of men stumbled into the alley just beyond. Two were still sober enough to be on their feet, while the third was being dragged between them. Judging from the sharp profanities ringing up from the valley, he was not a friend.

They threw him down in a pile of raw sewage and kicked him a few times before one of them pulled a bow from his back and shot the poor man right in the head. His body twitched twice then went perfectly still as they threw back their heads with laughter, heading back into the bar.

"Yeah," Asher murmured with a frown, "...lovely."

"This is a bad idea," Evie said quietly. "We should stick to the forest, try to—"

"Did you see that bow?"

She glanced up in surprise to see Ellanden still staring down at the valley, a look of open jealousy splashed across his face. Cosette was just a foot behind, looking exactly the same way.

"Are you serious?" she demanded, snapping her fingers in front of their faces. "We just saw a guy murdered in cold blood, and you're more interested in the bow?!"

Cosette winced apologetically, still unable to tear her eyes away. "It had a rosewood exterior—"

"Listen, Everly…" Ellanden held up both hands, obviously trying to project an air of practicality. "Those men who attacked us probably came from a place just like this, and there are undoubtedly more on the road. It would be…irresponsible of us *not* to go down there. We need to see what we're up against for ourselves. And gather supplies accordingly."

Cosette nodded behind him, her eyes as wide as saucers, but the others were in no way fooled. Asher, in particular, seemed to think it was an absolutely ludicrous idea. He glanced only once between the fae before crossing his arms with a withering glare.

"It would be *irresponsible*, would it?"

"Yes," Ellanden replied, nodding seriously, "quite."

"And it wouldn't have anything to do with you wanting that bow?"

There was a guilty pause as the fae's eyes flickered down to the clearing. "You see, Ash, when I said we should stock up on supplies, that sort of implied—"

"Weapons," the vampire muttered, shaking his head. "Yeah, I got it."

"Perfect." The prince smiled brightly, tucking his only remaining dagger into his belt. "So are we agreed? I'm sure at least one of those taverns has to have a vacancy…"

Evie and Asher shared an exasperated look before breaking with a grin. They were securing their own things a moment later. At this point, the princess really wished she was wearing clothes.

"So how exactly do you expect to purchase a room at one of these taverns if we don't have any money?" She pulled the clasp on her cloak as tight as it would go. "Are you going to sleep with the proprietor, or should I?"

"Well, that depends entirely on the proprietor," Ellanden answered practically.

Asher glanced up swiftly, but held his tongue. Just a quick look, but it was enough to catch the princess' eye. She sauntered over to him with a smile, pulling him a few steps away.

"I'm sorry...am I not supposed to make those kinds of jokes now that we're dating?"

Ellanden lifted his head curiously. "Was that a joke?"

"Not talking to you!" Evie called back before turning to the vampire with a sweet smile. "I could always tone it down a bit. Heaven forbid I make you fret."

He flashed a grin, pulling her closer by the hips. "Fret? Do I look like I'm fretting to you?"

"You look about a second away from kissing me," she breathed, tossing back her hair with a mischievous smile. "Not that I can blame you. After all, I *am* the girl who saved everyone from the kelpies. The same girl who freed you in a daring aquatic rescue, then saved you all over again by offering the blood from her very veins—"

"Yeah, I get it. You're a hero." He bent down and kissed her, soft as a dream. "You know, it occurs to me, I never did thank you for any of that."

She shrugged coyly, stretching up on her toes to steal another. "I can think of several ways you could thank me."

They kissed yet again, unable to stop.

"I could always get started right now," he teased, looking her up and down. "Do you happen to be naked under that cloak—"

"And *that's* all my gag reflex can handle," Ellanden declared, clapping his hands briskly before gesturing down the bluff. "Let's get a move on. The night's wasting."

The couple pulled apart with matching grins as the rest of them started heading down into the valley. Ellanden stood at the top, waving them along impatiently.

"*That's* all your gag reflex can handle?" Freya scoffed, marching past him. "You'd make a terrible girl..."

AS IT TURNED OUT, THE settlement wasn't nearly so bad as it had looked from a distance.

It was much, *much* worse.

Everywhere you looked, the place screamed danger. Oftentimes literally. There were swarms of roving goblins, packs of towering trolls. A lone banshee was sitting on an empty mead barrel, snacking on what looked suspiciously like a tray of human fingers. While a man with the legs of a spider was perched atop the local card house, ominously beckoning people inside.

But those were the creatures Evie was able to identify. There were many that she wasn't.

Upon their rescue from the sorcerer's cage, Cosette had warned the friends that the realm had changed in more ways than one. Not only had creatures of light becomes scarce and disbanded, but creatures of darkness had risen forth to take their place. Carpathians had come out of hiding, vampires moved freely about the land. She saw now, that was just the tip of the iceberg.

There were surely names for what she was seeing, but nothing leapt to mind. After only a few moments, they blended together into a single mindless terror—the kind of thing you'd read about in stories, but never see walking the streets in real life.

Beasts with blood-red eyes and clawed appendages roamed from one tavern to another. A pair of skeletal elk made their way slowly down the center of the road, dragging their antlers in the dust. There were changelings of all shapes and sizes, a clicking insectoid language that stung the ears.

As they stood there gawking, a cluster of wraithlike children swarmed past them in a little pack. Evie's first instinct was to reach out to them, to protectively spirit them away from such a place. Then the one in back glanced over its shoulder—revealing the face of a snake and a body of pure black smoke. It flashed a bloody smile before vanishing with the others down the street.

"What was the word you used?" Asher asked quietly, watching as the man with the spider legs picked up a passing warlock and tore him in two. "...lovely?"

Freya tried to answer but she was staring in morbid fascination at the banshee, looking like she was going to be sick.

Ellanden clapped a hand over her eyes, steering them towards the tavern. "Come on, let's get inside."

THE ONLY DIFFERENCE between the tavern and the streets beyond was that one happened to be indoors. Aside from that, everything remained exactly the same. The level of noise, the casual displays of destruction. But most importantly, the clientele.

The friends ducked inside then froze, watching as girl with spiked tentacles seized a passing shifter and smashed him repeatedly into the wall. A nearby succubus nodded approvingly, muttering about promises of monogamy as the shifter in question dripped back down to the floor.

"New plan," Freya whispered, turning around to face the others. "I vote that we march straight back to the forest and find a different way to get to the Dunes."

The others were tempted to agree with her, but found themselves shaking their heads.

"These people didn't come from nowhere," Asher murmured, ducking as a half-full bottle of scotch went flying his way. "The whole middle country must be full of them. I hate to say it, but the fae are right. If we want to stand a chance out there, we'll need to arm up."

There was a piercing wail from the other side of the tavern, followed by a splash of blood.

"Tomorrow," Ellanden clarified quickly, making a bee-line for the bar. "We'll find some weapons tomorrow. In the meantime, I suggest we get the hell out of the way."

The princess couldn't agree with him more. It wouldn't take much to lose one's head in such a crowd. Tempers were high, patience was scarce. And everyone had consumed enough alcohol that if one were to simply light a match, there was a chance the entire place might explode.

All the more reason to get to bed.

"Excuse me?" Ellanden leaned across the counter, catching the bartender's eye. "Who do I speak with about acquiring a room for the night?"

His beauty was enough to get him noticed, but the reputation of the fae provided some degree of protection as well. The other patrons glanced up curiously, but left him well enough alone.

The bartender, who appeared to be some sort of squid, rapped blindly on the wall behind him, mixing a constant stream of drinks with his other arms. A moment later, a bustling man in an apron stepped out behind the bar. He appeared normal enough, except he was ten feet tall.

"What is it?" he demanded, busy and impatient to have been disturbed. The squid-man made some series of beeps in reply, and he turned with sudden interest to the gang. "So, you're interested in purchasing a room for the evening?"

Ellanden blinked quickly, then nodded his head. "Yes, are you the man to speak with about that?"

"Sure am."

The man pointed to a sign above him, listing prices. The fae glanced up then emptied the contents of his pocket into the man's hand. It was the only coin the group had left—stolen off the body of one of the men from the caravan. They stared after it nervously, aching to take it back.

"You got yourself a room," the man said with a smile, handing the fae a key. "I even put you on the top story, just in case."

Just in case? Was it somehow safer on the top story?

Her eyes flickered to the ceiling, while Ellanden flashed a tight smile.

"Thank you—"

"Stay a while," the man interrupted, catching his arm. "You have a room, now why don't you get yourself a drink? I'm sure there are plenty of people down here who'd love to share the company of such..." His eyes swept over the friends. "...an interesting group of people."

Interesting? If it wasn't so terrifying, Evie would have laughed. *He works in THIS place day in and out, and he thinks that WE'RE the interesting ones?*

Only later would she realize the chilling truth. In such a place, amidst a crowd of such deadly creatures, the little gang of companions stood out more than they would ever know.

Ellanden smiled again, casually extracting his arm. "Perhaps another time. We've travelled a long way. All we really want now is a bed."

"Suit yourselves," the proprietor chuckled, his eyes lingering as they vanished quickly up the stairs. "To be honest, it's probably for the best..."

The friends took the steps five at a time, not daring to look down behind them. They'd almost reached the top of the stairs, when Asher cleared his throat softly, ducking onto the fourth-floor landing instead. With a little wink, he pulled a key from his pocket and opened the door.

"What is this?" Evie asked in astonishment as she and the others filed past him. "I thought we were at the top—"

"About fifteen people heard the guy say he put us at the top story," Asher replied, locking the door safely behind them. "And by 'people' I mean whatever was drinking in that bar."

She folded her arms with a shiver, watching as he and Ellanden dragged the wooden dresser across the floor, wedging it firmly against the rusted doorframe.

"What about the windows?" Freya asked with wide eyes. All the excitement from the bluff had vanished now that she'd actually seen the encampment up close. "Should we prop up the bed in front of them, or—"

"The windows would be our way out," Ellanden cut her off, with an easy smile. "And you don't have to worry about any of that. Ash and I will be keeping watch. You just get some sleep."

Any other day, the witch would have argued. Any other day Evie would have rolled her eyes and Cosette would have sharply reminded him that they were perfectly capable of keeping watch themselves. But there were only a few hours until morning. And they desperately needed to sleep.

"If you're sure," she said brightly, jumping into bed. A second later she reconsidered, eyeing the mattress doubtfully before settling on the floor instead. "You'll get no protest from me."

Cosette settled down beside her, the blade of a dagger gripped snugly in her hand, while Evie stepped lightly over them and joined the boys at the window. Ellanden was already in his own world, staring in dark fascination at the chaos happening below. Asher's attention was a bit more directed.

"What are you looking at?" she murmured, resting her chin on his shoulder.

He gestured silently and she followed his gaze.

Two people in dark cloaks were cutting swiftly through the bustling streets, keeping an even stride as the crowd parted before them like water. It was difficult to see much beneath their heavy hoods, but there was something strangely familiar about the way they carried themselves. Like they were floating instead of walking. Almost like—

"Are they vampires?" she whispered, stiffening in alarm.

In hindsight, she wished she hadn't been leaning against him. He surely felt it when her muscles tensed involuntarily. Just like he heard the secret panic hidden beneath the words.

"Yep," he said quietly, eyes never leaving them. A strange expression washed over him, followed by an even quieter sigh. "Of course you'd find vampires in a place like this."

Ellanden flashed him a quick glance before attempting to lighten the mood. "Look around and you'll also find witches and fae." He cocked his head 'discreetly' towards Evie. "Not to mention a badly-trained wolf I've been meaning to speak with you about."

The princess elbowed him sharply, while Asher flashed a faint smile. The vampires were gone now, vanished through the door of a tavern. Who knew what havoc they might wreak inside.

"All this...and our parents still left."

The teasing abruptly faded as the others stared out the window as well. It was the thing none of them had been saying. The silent burden weighing constantly on their minds.

Never in a thousand years would such a thing have been allowed to exist under the reign of the young monarchs. They would have delighted in destroying it, doing so with such wild abandon that others would speak of it for years to come. No other such beasts would dare to assemble. The encampment would have been disassembled, allowing the previous tenants to reclaim the land.

"When Cosette saw this place, she didn't look surprised," Ellanden murmured softly. "When Freya was talking about the raiders who killed her adoptive parents, she didn't sound surprised." He stared a moment longer before turning to the others. "How could they have done it? How could they have given back the crown...and just left the kingdoms to tear themselves apart?"

Evie's eyes hardened as she gazed out the window.

Since waking up from that enchanted sleep, she'd asked herself the same question. The more places they'd travelled, the more things they'd seen, the heavier it seemed to weigh. A part of her kept thinking there had to be some mitigating circumstance. A spell, or explosion, or *anything at all* that would explain her parents' sudden exodus from the realm. They might not often admit it, they might have even lied if asked outright...but they loved sitting at the helm of the five kingdoms.

And it wasn't just the people or the crown—they loved the responsibility. They loved being able to call the shots instead of being forced to watch things deteriorate at the mercy of others. The realm was precious to them, and there was no one they'd trust better to protect it than themselves.

So why did they walk away?

Evie stared another moment out the window before turning to her friends. "We're going to ask them. We're going to ask them that question ourselves."

She didn't know when, she didn't know how. By the time they completed their fateful quest, it was very likely not all of them would be alive to do so. But that question needed an answer.

They would find a way.

"Now get some sleep," she finished abruptly. "I'll take first watch."

Chapter 11

After witnessing how the encampment transformed after a night of heavy drinking, the five friends thought things would have surely calmed down in the morning.

They were dead wrong. Again.

The second they stepped outside, they were forced to jump back to avoid getting crushed by the falling body of a recently-decapitated troll. It fell in front of them with a sickening *thump*, sending up a spray of viscera and dust. They blinked in a daze, then slowly lifted their heads as a dwarf carrying a blood-stained battle-axe walked past them, dragging the blade in the sand.

He saw them looking almost immediately and turned to face them square on. The axe twirled on the ground beside him. Little pieces were still lodged in the troll's neck.

For a split second, nothing happened. Then Freya waved with a beaming smile.

The dwarf rolled his eyes and swung the axe over his shoulder, muttering under his breath as he headed off down the lane. Not until he'd rounded the bend did the rest of them pull in a breath.

Well...that bodes well.

The scene probably should have made more of an impact, but the friends were running low on sleep. The deafening noise filtering up from the bar was enough to contend with on its own, and it certainly hadn't helped that halfway through the night there had been a hushed commotion on the stairwell as a group of unseen creatures ghosted past them to the top story. There had been a scrape of metal as the lock was picked. A hushed profanity when they saw the room was empty.

The friends had listened breathlessly from below, eyes fixed on the ceiling. The window was hanging open. If the creatures decided to continue the search, they'd have no choice but to jump.

Needless to say, it had already been a long day. And the day had only gotten started.

Evie stepped gingerly over the fallen carcass, careful not to get any arterial detritus on the hem of her cloak. Unlike the others she still had yet to find any real clothing, and the success of the morning's ventures would affect her more than most. That being said, they had a slight problem.

"So what's the plan?" she asked shortly, turning to face the others. "We have no coin, no credit, and we came here looking to buy. What are we going to do?"

Asher elbowed Ellanden back to attention, forcing his eyes away from the headless troll.

"Sorry—what?"

Evie folded her arms tightly, securing her cloak at the same time.

"What are we going to do about *money*?" she asked again, more impatiently. "You know I hate to insist, but since I appear to be one of only *three* women in this entire settlement, and I also happen to have lost all my *clothes*..."

She stressed each word dangerously and the fae was quick to nod.

"Yes, I have a plan for that."

Fortunately, his plan chose that moment to make a sudden appearance.

The gang turned around as the tavern door opened and the proprietor who'd rented them the room wandered out onto the front stoop. He was whistling cheerfully, hands in his pockets, and about had a heart attack when he glanced down and saw the friends staring up at him.

"Oh!" he gasped, clutching at his chest. "Good—good morning!"

Evie's eyes narrowed and Asher's face went suddenly cold.

Didn't expect to see us again, did you?

"I hope the room was acceptable," he stammered nervously, eyes flickering between the vampire and the fae. "The bar can be quite loud—"

Ellanden crossed the distance between them, gazing up with a hard smile. The man might have been over ten feet tall, but there wasn't a doubt in anyone's mind what the fae was capable of.

"Actually, we didn't end up needing the room after all." With that, he pressed not one but two keys into the man's hand, maintaining direct eye contact the entire time. "Given that information, I'm sure you'll agree that a full refund is in order."

A subtle threat was one thing. The transfer of money was another.

The polite façade vanished as the man looked at him appraisingly, glancing every so often at the people standing by his side. It was a strange bunch—he'd noted that the previous evening. And the presence of a vampire was more than enough to make him pause.

After a moment of silent deliberation, he flashed what could pass as a courteous smile.

"Of course." He rummaged in his pocket a moment before producing the same coins the fae had surrendered the night before. "And I do hope you'll consider staying with us again."

Don't count on it.

The friends waited until he'd gone inside before coming together in a huddle, dividing the money quickly as they started making plans.

"The main thing is weapons," Evie said practically. While each of them had their own set of supernatural defenses, there was no underestimating the value of a good blade. "Knives, bows, swords—some kind of hatchet for making fires. Don't worry about things like food, as there was plenty of game in the woods. But if anyone happens to see some blankets or a tent..."

The men nodded silently, scanning the stores around them.

"What about bandages?" Freya asked practically.

The princess glanced down at the sum in front of her, then shook her head.

"If anyone gets injured, we'll just cut off that limb. Agreed?"

"Agreed," the rest chorused back to her.

"That's a lot to buy with very little coin," Cosette murmured, turning over the few bronze pieces she held in her hand. "Is it going to be enough?"

"It will be if we're careful," Asher assured her, trying not to worry himself. "And with a little creative bargaining on our parts."

The fae princess sighed, tying back her long hair.

"There's no need to bargain," she said softly, lifting a hand to her neck. "Not while I—"

"You're not selling that," Ellanden interrupted swiftly, swatting down her hand before she could expose the necklace of jewels underneath. "I won't permit it."

Evie pursed her lips, while Freya openly grinned. The fae's ages might have shifted, but the dynamic between them hadn't changed. At least not in Ellanden's mind.

Cosette was a slightly different story.

"Oh...you won't *permit* it?" Her eyebrows lifted dangerously as she placed her hands on her hips.

"No," he stated, leaning down with the hint of a grin, "I won't. Now why don't you run along and see if you can find us a hatchet. Think you can handle that, kid?"

She flashed a sweet smile, then head-butted him right in the nose. "I'll manage."

He grinned affectionately, staring after her, then frowned with brotherly concern at the men watching her weave through the crowd. His knuckles tightened on the handle of his knife before he visibly restrained himself, nudging the vampire instead.

"Ash, do you think—"

"I'm on it."

He was gone a moment later, slipping after her in the crowd.

And then there were three.

It felt like madness to split up, but the encampment was a sprawling wasteland. And unless they wanted to spend another night at the tavern, they needed to find what they required and leave.

"So where does that leave us?" Freya asked, looking secretly pleased that the fae had stayed behind. "Swords, or knives, or—"

"Bows," Evie and Ellanden answered at the same time.

They shared a quick grin. The princess might have restrained herself in wake of the moonlit homicide they'd witnessed the night before, but she'd been just as excited as the fae by the choice of weapon. It had been a long time since she'd felt the smooth curve of wood beneath her fingers. And the way she figured, if anyone deserved a reward for recent services it was her.

They couldn't always expect her to fend off their attackers as a dog.

"Naturally," Freya said with false enthusiasm, trailing behind as they made their way excitedly through the crowd. "The one weapon I don't know how to use..."

FOUR HOURS LATER, THE friends met back at the same bar. The sun had risen directly overhead and they were all in fine spirits, having completed their assignments with glowing success.

"That's walnut on the grip, ironwood on the riser." Ellanden traced his fingers tenderly along the edge of his new bow, cradling the thing like it was a newborn child. "Perfectly balanced, but you expect that from Becatti craftsmen. And weighted *just* enough to make it really sing."

Freya banged her head theatrically against the table, while Asher stifled a smile.

"You fae talk about archery the way my people talk about blood. It's a little creepy."

Ellanden ignored him, still reveling in his prize. "Just feel it," he said proudly, extending the bow across the table. "Not a single seam in the wood. I swear, the thing's bloomin' near perfect."

"You want to say it a little louder?" Asher teased, running his finger obligingly over the gentle curve. "I don't think those warlocks heard you at the other end of the bar. Those shifters definitely did. And they'd be more than happy to take it off your hands."

"Let them try," Ellanden answered haughtily, feeling far more confident in the strange encampment now that he was armed. "It'll give me a chance to christen this beauty."

Normally, Evie would have jumped right on the bandwagon teasing him, but both she and Cosette happened to be reveling in weapons of their own. They'd both gotten bows, of course. But in a last-second decision, Evie had decided to forgo her traditional pair of knives and spend the coin on a sword instead. She had training in both. The friends had training in everything. But a sudden feeling of nostalgia swept over her the moment she saw the blade. It wasn't as ostentatious as the others, but it was very finely made. The weapon a ranger might carry. It reminded her of her father's.

"Beauty, huh?" Asher lifted his eyebrows. "And how much did this beauty cost?"

Ellanden innocently glanced away, pretending not to hear him.

"In his defense," Evie interjected, "he got it at a *vastly* reduced price."

Of course, there was a reason for that. The fae had waited until the man who ran the shop was busy before appealing to the pretty salesgirl instead. Things had progressed from there.

Freya's eyes flashed as she banged a hand upon the table. "Are we going to get some food or what? We have a little coin left over."

The others quickly agreed, if for no other reason than to avoid the shower of sparks that followed, and the two men got up together to place their order at the bar.

"You're being *really* obvious, you know."

Evie glanced up in surprise to see Cosette looking steadily across the table. The witch flushed in response, but immediately busied herself with her cloak.

"What do you mean—"

"He's not a good idea. He's not a good choice."

This time, the implication was too obvious to ignore. Freya's fingers hovered over the fabric before she gave up the ghost, folding them neatly on the table.

"It doesn't hurt to look."

"As long as looking is all you do," Cosette cautioned. "The guy didn't get that reputation of his by chance, Freya. He's not exactly looking to settle down."

"Maybe I'm not either—"

"Maybe you're not *listening*," Cosette interrupted with a hint of impatience. "He sees you as a kid, Freya. As that same little kid who ran screaming from a witch's cottage. The one he left in a candy shop before going off to save the world. It doesn't matter how much time has passed. That's what you are to him. That's all the two of you are ever going to be."

Freya's eyes sparked, then cooled almost simultaneously. "It's a good thing I'm not invested, then."

"Yeah, it's a good thing."

The table fell silent for a few moments, then Evie leaned forward with a frown.

"Wait—are you guys talking about Ellanden?"

The girls flashed her an identical look before turning back to their drinks.

"You're hopeless."

"Seven hells..."

The conversation had been deliberately closed by the time the men returned to the table, catching their fair share of looks from other patrons in the bar. It wasn't often one saw a fae and a vampire travelling together. When they sat down at a table of lovely women, it was hard to ignore.

Already, the whispers were starting.

A trio of shifters bowed their heads together, talking preferences while shooting sideways glances at the women. The girl with the tentacles from the night before was making eyes at Asher, oblivious to the fact that there were still drops of blood on her face. Goblins spoke secretly, while dwarves laughed openly at bawdy jokes. But perhaps the most unsettling was when a pair of what looked like person-sized beetles clicked at each other before burying their heads in a plate full of sand.

Evie was still gawking incredulously, when a sudden movement caught her eye. A table of creatures heavily draped in thick cloaks was conversing on the other side of the bar. As she was looking one of them turned slowly, staring straight at her with a pair of dark, soulless eyes—

A hand smacked her upside the head.

"Don't antagonize the ghouls," Ellanden chided.

Holy crap...is that what those are?

No matter what ghastly creatures may have surrounded him, the fae was in unbreakable high spirts. Evie suspected this had a great deal to do with his new bow. She wouldn't be surprised if he slept with it under his pillow that night.

The others were a bit more on edge. Particularly, the vampire.

"So are we to continue heading west?" he asked quietly, trying to ignore a pair of glittering eyes watching him from the corner. "The owner of the shop where we purchased the tent said there were two main trails apart from the main road—"

"Might as well take the main road," Ellanden said confidently, downing what was left of his whiskey and imagining himself shooting down the bar's patrons, one by one. "If you ask me, we've been playing defense a little too long—"

"Be serious," Asher interrupted sharply. "The sooner we leave this place behind us, the better. I don't know if you remember, but we happen to be in a bit of a hurry—"

"I'm sorry to hear that."

The friends looked up with a start as a pair of tall men appeared suddenly beside their table, staring down with the same silky smile. It took Evie a moment to realize they were the ones who'd been watching from the corner. It took another moment to realize what they were.

"Hello, child."

Asher stiffened under their intense gaze. He alone didn't seem surprised to see them. He simply wished the gang had left the bar before the introduction had a chance to occur.

Instead of answering, he nodded curtly. Providing no further openings.

The vampires smiled again.

"Hardly a sign of respect, young one. Though you're right to be cautious." The one who had spoken cast a quick look around the tavern before catching him once more in that curious gaze. "It wasn't our intention to disturb your meal, but it's strange to see one of our kind travelling around on his own. Especially one so young as yourself."

How can they tell? Evie had always wondered.

"I'm not alone," Asher replied stiffly, though he seemed hesitant to call attention to his friends. "I'm travelling with companions."

The vampire smiled again, enjoying their little exchange.

"A sight that's even stranger still."

A whisper of sound passed between them, almost like they were scenting the air.

"Would you mind if we joined you? Only for a moment, of course." The vampire's dark eyes rested a moment on the fae before sparkling with an inviting smile. "We'd love to hear about your travels, buy you the next round of drinks—"

"Thank you," Asher said quickly, "but we were just on our way out."

The others pushed silently to their feet, tensing involuntarily as the vampires' eyes rested on each of them in turn. Cosette's hand was on her dagger. Ellanden was itching to reach for his bow.

But what happened next was in the hands of the vampires.

Only they could decide how the game would be played.

For a suspended moment, it looked as though they were considering. Judging by the ease of their stance, they were confident about their chances. And their eyes dilated hungrily as they flashed once more to the fae. But the sight of Asher standing in between made them reconsider.

"In that case...don't let us delay you."

They parted at the same time, moving so suddenly that wisps of Evie's hair blew away from her face. At first glance, it was even more terrifying. In order to leave the table, each friend would have to pass in between. But when Asher stepped boldly through the middle the others followed suit, shooting wary glances to the side as they made their way quickly through the tavern.

They were almost to the door when the vampire who'd been speaking called softly through the crowd. The words were lost on the rest of the patrons. But Asher heard them loud and clear.

"Have a care as to your friends, young one. And have a care as to your enemies as well."

Asher glanced over his shoulder and their eyes met for a suspended moment.

"We'll be seeing you again."

***

BY THE TIME THE FRIENDS left the tavern, those 'fine spirits' of theirs had vanished on a dime.

Evie and Freya were doing their best to hold back over-inquisitive questions, Cosette and Ellanden kept casting involuntary looks over their shoulders, and Asher was staring blankly ahead—wishing they'd never decided to travel on the main road.

With no instructions other than to head west the gang made their way in silence through the winding encampment, picking up pace as the sun began to drop lower in the scorching sky. Clouds of dust hung heavy in the air around them. Any grass that might have grown in the valley had been trampled to extinction under so many pairs of careless feet.

After a few minutes, Ellanden made a brave attempt to break the silence. Granted, he did so in a particularly exasperating way.

"...could have shot them both with my bow..."

"Enough with the bow!" Asher snapped, throwing up his hands in a sudden flare of temper, as if he'd simply needed a push to start shouting himself. "No one cares about the damn bow!"

The fae wisely held his tongue, but the vampire wasn't finished.

"And no, you could not have *shot* them, Ellanden. Those two were almost as old as my father. They would have ripped you in half."

The fae's jaw twitched, as if he was dying to refute it, but before he could speak Evie lay a restraining hand upon his arm. The moment came and went as she looked at Asher imploringly.

"Yes, but...how did you *know* they were that old?"

The others were quick to chime in themselves.

"That's exactly what I was going to ask."

"They didn't look any older than thirty."

"...definitely could have got them with my bow."

Asher threw up his hands again, laughing manically under his breath.

"You're all incorrigible! Tell me again why I didn't let them eat you all on the spot!"

There was a beat of silence. Then Ellanden bit his lip.

"Because I would have shot—"

This time Asher leapt upon him with a genuine grin, trying to wrestle it out of his hands. "I'm going to strangle you with that bow—"

"Now *that* would be a waste."

For the second time, the friends whirled around to see a man watching them from the chair of an outdoor café. Five empty goblets littered the table in front of him, but he didn't look remotely intoxicated. If anything, the small barrel of whiskey seemed to sharpen his gaze.

As they were looking, he pushed slowly to his feet. And kept going and going. By the time he was standing, it became clear they were looking at the only thing worse than a vampire.

...that's a Carpathian.

"Not too many fae left in the world," he continued, with what might have passed as a friendly smile if it weren't so frightening. "You can't go around strangling them on a whim."

Asher tried to move them forward, but Ellanden was rooted to the spot. Many times had they heard of such men, but when the friends were still children the infamous horde had been driven from the known world. Hunted down to near extinction. Believed to be completely lost.

And this man was sipping whiskey at a roadside café.

The man tilted his head with a smile, studying the fae right back. His eyes flickered over every inch before coming to rest on the bow strapped to his back.

"That's if you could manage it." He flashed a crooked grin. "They're also hard to kill."

Ellanden made a compulsive movement, whitening with rage.

The man was a head taller and twice his size—with a chest the size of a barrel and bulging arms each wider than the princess' legs. Unfortunately, none of that seemed to matter. The prince had killed a basilisk and he was freshly armed. Fae also weren't known for keeping their temper.

"And what would you know of it?" he hissed.

The man smiled broadly, closing the distance between them in a single step.

"I've had plenty of experience with your kind," he answered. "I fought at the Battle of Alenforth. Got to see it all with my own eyes."

Ellanden stiffened dramatically. Evie remembered studying the battle as well.

Of all the assaults and skirmishes in the months after the Dunes, Alenforth had been one of the bloodiest. A company of Fae cavalry had gone up against an entire brigade of Carpathians, trying to drive them from an ancestral forest. The fae had been victorious, but it had taken time. After the initial assault, the next several days were spent hunting the Carpathians still hiding in the woods.

"I'm surprised you're here to talk about it," Ellanden said coldly. "I was under the impression most of your kind was wiped out."

The man tilted his head with that same frightening smile.

"Plenty of your kind, too. Some by my own hand." He stroked his chin, eyes glittering at the thought. "I remember this one fae in particular—kept firing off arrows as my battalion retreated in front of him—a truly masterful shot. He got about thirty of them before I tackled him off his horse and plunged a knife into his side. Normally, I would have just killed him and been done with it, but the rest of the cavalry was already leaving, and my people were fleeing into the woods."

As he spoke, he pulled a savage-looking knife from the loop of his belt. The jagged blade was almost as long as Evie's arm. He twirled it casually as he continued to speak.

"I dragged him into a cave instead—waited until the last of the fighters were gone. Fae heal quickly, so I had to keep reopening the wound. That wasn't hard, given how much he struggled."

Faster and faster the knife spun, glinting in the dying sun.

"Three days I kept him there. A butterfly in a cage. Did all sorts of terrible things to him. Then the morning of the fourth day, I went into the cave. You wouldn't believe what happened."

The blade stopped abruptly, just inches from Ellanden's face.

"Let me guess," the fae muttered. "You killed him."

The Carpathian shook his head, slipping the knife back into its sheath. "He'd hanged himself."

For whatever reason, this stung worst of all.

Evie blinked several times, feeling suddenly cold. Even Ellanden was so unnerved by the sudden ending that he didn't even see the man getting closer until it was too late.

"The thing is, you look an awful lot like him—"

The prince let out a vile oath, drawing a blade as the man stroked a finger down his face. It flashed in the air between them, but a moment before it could hit Asher caught him by the wrist.

"Not here," he cautioned quietly. "Not like this."

Ellanden thrashed violently against his restraining hands, but the Carpathian was already walking away. Saluting with the last of the whiskey and chuckling under his breath.

"Listen to your friend. You wouldn't want to lose that pretty head."

The fae cursed again as he disappeared, then turned on the vampire in a rage.

"What the hell were you thinking?!" he demanded, wrenching his arm away. "I *had* him—"

"Possibly," Asher panted, gesturing back to the tavern. "And what were you going to do when that bar emptied and a mob of drunken mercenaries poured onto the street? Were you going to fight all of them, too? Have the rest of us fight them?"

Ellanden's dark eyes swept quickly over the others. Then he turned in the direction the Carpathian had disappeared, still clutching hard to the handle of his knife.

"The man was a monster. He deserved to die." He stared a second longer before turning those burning eyes to Asher. "You should have let me kill him."

"There's always tomorrow," Asher tempered quietly, leading him the opposite way. "At any rate, the last thing we want to do in a place like this is cause trouble..."

But trouble had a way of finding them.

And they wouldn't have long to wait.

Chapter 12

They had *almost* left the settlement. They had *almost* made it back to the road. Then a massive cheer rose up from the outdoor arena and they stopped in their tracks.

"No," Asher said preemptively, reading the others' faces with a familiar dismay. "I know what you're thinking—but no."

Evie and Ellanden exchanged a quick look before turning to the arena.

"But aren't you the least bit curious?" she asked, trying to see past the milling crowd to the other side of the street. "Not even the least?"

"It could be helpful," Ellanden added practically. "We don't know anything about the power dynamic in this part of the realm, and every bit of knowledge helps."

"Those are your arguments?" Asher's eyes narrowed as his arms folded tightly across his chest. "Aren't you curious and the power of knowledge?"

There was a beat of silence.

"...it could also be fun?"

With a sigh of frustration, the vampire turned to Cosette. "Your cousin's deranged. Help me out here."

She merely shrugged, rubbing a layer of polish over her new bow. "I wouldn't mind checking it out."

"I *also* want to go," Freya chimed in. "If that counts for anything."

"Absolutely," Ellanden replied immediately, wrapping an arm around her shoulders. "We operate based on the needs of the majority. That's four to one, Ash." She shifted her weight, still adjusting to the new clothes on her cloak.

The vampire threw up his hands in exasperation, but after so many years he'd grown used to a certain degree of whimsical recklessness from the other two. Before he could try again to dissuade them, another mighty cheer rose up from the arena and a rabid excitement lit their eyes.

At that point, there was no stopping them.

"Don't worry, babe. It's going to be fun!" Evie slipped her hand into his, tugging him down the street. "We'll only stay a minute and then we'll get right back on the road, I promise."

He started with another caustic retort, then glanced at her in surprise. "Did you just call me 'babe'?"

She froze guilty. "...no."

It was perhaps for this reason and no other that the vampire kept his complaints to himself and reluctantly followed after the others as they joined the mob of creatures surging to the arena.

In a way, it was the most dangerous thing they'd done yet. In a crowd of drunken monsters and supernatural misfits, the five friends were often the smallest things around. They hadn't been walking more than a few minutes before an ogre lost his balance and crushed the three dwarves walking behind him. Not long after that a slimy creature with bat-like wings pulled out a rapier, accidentally decapitating the warlock who was right alongside.

With each new disaster, Asher's patience got a little thinner.

With each new disaster, Evie squeezed his hand a little more.

When at last they burst through a set of tall wooden doors, the princess was surprised to see that they were still outside. The arena was nothing more than a roped off circle in the middle of a wide open field. The encampment was on one side, the woods that led to the western trail were on another. She was about to point out how convenient this was to the vampire, when there was a collective gasp and a reptilian head flew out of the arena, skidding to a stop at her feet.

Okay...maybe not my best idea.

For a split second, all was quiet. Then the crowd exploded in applause.

A grimlock swooped out of nowhere, throwing it over the stands where the rest of the audience proceeded to bat it around like a ball, ignoring the ribbons of greenish slime flinging about in its wake. They surged and shrieked with feral screams, each leaping up for a chance to strike.

The friends stared another moment, then Ellanden gestured to the woods.

"Oh look—the western trail. Shall we?"

The vampire gave him a dry look. "Indeed."

Together, the five of them moved quickly off the wooden risers, making their way through the tall grass. It was slow work, given how many people were milling about—flagons of ale affixed permanently to their hands. There were several awkward run-ins, several muttered apologies as they hurried through. They were still in the thick of things when a ringing voice echoed over the crowd.

"Let's hear it again for our champion! Still undefeated, after all this time!"

Another deafening roar echoed up from the stands and the friends turned around in spite of themselves, curious to see what sort of beast could make such a claim...only to freeze in shock.

"I don't believe it," Freya gasped, her eyes as wide as saucers. "Is that—"

"It can't be," Asher murmured, but he didn't look so sure.

"But it is!" Evie cried in amazement. "That's the same shifter from the bar! The one who—"

She stopped herself suddenly, hand clamped over her mouth.

...the one who kissed Cosette.

The fae princess was standing frozen beside her, staring through the crowd like she'd seen a ghost. There was no telling how much she'd thought of the man since their fateful encounter. But judging by the look on her face, it was safe to say he'd crossed her mind.

After today, he was bound to make an impression.

No sooner had one fight ended than another begun. The shifter was still standing in the center of the ring, hands lifted to the crowd, when a shadowy creature leapt over the side—a pair of glittering scythes in his hands. There was no time for adjustment. No time to acknowledge the dark spirit streaking towards him, wielding the traditional weapons of death. The moment the monster crossed the rope the shifter charged forward himself, twirling a battered sword above his head.

It was almost too gruesome to watch, but the princess couldn't tear her eyes away. If she was being honest—though it cost her no small amount of pride—the sight reminded her of one of the sparring sessions back at the castle. Where one of their parents would hang up their cloak of royal propriety and challenge another in the ring.

The guy's skill was unbelievable. Even fighting with an inferior weapon, it was easy to see why he'd lasted in the arena so long. When the scythes flashed towards him, he parried. When the creature grew frustrated with conventional weapons and discarded them in favor of a pair of vicious curling claws, he adjusted his strategy as well. Keeping the fight bizarrely airborne as he danced and vaulted around the arena, occasionally flipping over the creature's head.

There was a control that spoke to years of experience, though Evie had seen for herself that he was very young. There was a quiet wisdom, executed with such reckless abandon he would have met even the most exact royal standards and made their relentless teachers proud.

She knew a certain Belarian king who would have appreciated the talent.

Personally, she was blown away.

As the fight continued, it became clear he was just stalling—playing to the excitement of the crowd. What was an arena match, after all, if not an exhibition?

The creature would be allowed to make some terrifying progress before he'd drive it back with a fury. He would teeter on the brink of failure before dazzling them in yet another display of impossible skill. At one point the man actually slowed down his moves, giving the audience time to catch up with what was happening. All the while, money was switching hands.

Seven hells...

Faster and faster they went. One of them, biding his time. The other, losing all semblance of control or dignity as it threw back its cloak with a series of enraged little snarls. The crowd began to laugh as the shifter lifted his eyebrows, taking a step back for the first time.

"Well, *that* is thoroughly disgusting," he said conversationally, looking past the cloak to the mottled nightmarish creature underneath. "What are you exactly?"

The beast flew towards him once, firing off an arch of acidic spray. The shifter dodged it quickly, striking it back again with the base of his sword.

"Or should I say, what *were* you," he amended apologetically. "It already smells as though you recently died."

There was another roar of laughter, but the match had apparently come to an end.

Evie watched with interest as one of the men standing alongside the rope lifted his hand in a discreet signal. The shifter caught the gesture and threw himself forward, finishing the fight at once.

There was surprisingly little fanfare. Given his previous posturing, Evie wouldn't have been at all surprised to discover that he'd been the one to throw the reptile's head into the crowd. But it took little more than a cursory examination to see his breathtaking performance was simply that.

A performance.

As the creature crumbled to oblivion and a shower of coins flew down into the arena he turned to face the open field, wiping the blade of his sword with a look of disgust.

The crowd never noticed. The friends pulled in their first breath.

"That's...unlikely." Ellanden stared a split second longer, then turned on his heel. "Well, no point in dawdling. Shall we get to the trail—"

"Landi," Asher chided quietly. "The last time we saw the guy, he was running into a burning building to attack a pack of shifters with nothing but an axe. *His* pack of shifters. And that was after he took the fall for something we did, just to help so the rest of us could escape."

Ellanden stared blankly. "...and?"

The vampire closed his eyes, trying hard to be patient. "And perhaps we owe him the courtesy of a thank-you before fleeing into the forest?"

"The man was trying to *rob* us," Ellanden retorted, looking highly offended the idea was even being discussed. "Now you want us to go *thank* him?"

"I want us to practice some basic human decency, yes."

"Human decency—"

"And *don't* say that neither of us is strictly human," the vampire cut him off. "Seven hells, Ellanden, it's a miracle no one ever strangled you in your sleep."

Evie held up her hands, turning to Cosette. "What would you like to do?"

The young fae froze, torn between the arena and her friends. For a moment, she looked almost tempted. Then her eyes drifted to Ellanden's impatient face.

"...I'd like to leave."

"See—of course she would!" The prince flashed her an indulgent smile before gesturing to the trail. "She's always been smart for her age. Now, you add ten years of experience to that..."

But as it turned out, the decision wasn't theirs to make.

Because the shifter had seen them at the same time.

"I thought it was you!"

In a flash the crowd parted as the young man came through, closing swiftly behind him as their attention turned to something else. He looked just as Evie remembered, only wearing fewer clothes. Tall and lean with sculpted muscles. A beautiful face and the bronzed skin of someone who'd been fighting the last few weeks in the sun. Most telling were his eyes. The guy might have been dripping trails of green monster blood, but his eyes were still sparkling.

"Don't tell me you're leaving already—the party's just begun!"

In what would later be described as an act of betrayal, four pairs of eyes shot at once to Cosette. The girl was frozen exactly where she'd been standing, one foot still angled to the trail.

"We were just…" She trailed off, looking uncharacteristically unsure. "We didn't—"

"We were just seeing what all the commotion was," Ellanden cut in smoothly, stepping between them. He clearly hadn't forgotten the shifter's rocky introduction, any more than he'd forgiven that stolen kiss. "But as it happens, we're in a bit of a hurry—"

"Would you like to fight?" the man offered quickly, gesturing back towards the arena. "One quick conversation and I could have you standing in that ring."

Ellanden froze in surprise, glancing over in spite of himself.

A layer of sawdust was being sprinkled over the grass to soak up the blood. A grotesquely undervalued gremlin trailed after, sweeping away the bones of all the people who had come before.

The fae was *aching* to try.

"Well, I suppose—" He caught his friends' incredulous look, and stopped himself quickly. "I mean, we don't fight for sport. But enjoy yourself. Try not to die."

The gang turned to leave, but in an act of recklessness unparalleled by anything that had come before the shifter grabbed the prince by the arm.

"Come on—I could get high odds against a fae," he coaxed with a smile. "When I win, I'll split the earnings with you. Seventy-thirty."

How generous.

Evie bit back a smile as the fae's eyebrows lifted to his hair. She noticed the shifter hadn't even mentioned the vampire. Perhaps those odds were a bit too high for even his tastes.

"*Really*, a whole thirty percent." Ellanden looked vaguely amused. "And if I win?"

The shifter's eyes travelled over the prince to the lovely girl behind him. They rested there a moment before twinkling with a secret smile. "If you win...then I promise to be a perfect gentleman when I take that one out to dinner."

There was a beat of silence.

"All right—I'll fight him."

Asher stepped quickly in between as the fae shed his cloak. The arena be damned. He was ready to tear the guy to pieces right there on the grass.

"*Or* we could get to the trail like we were planning," he cautioned, lowering his voice. "We could also remember what we said about keeping a low profile."

Ellanden nodded distractedly, but his eyes were fixed on the shifter. "Do you have a name? Or do they just give you numbers in this sort of thing"

The guy's smile faltered, but despite the previous teasing he seemed determined to be friendly. "It's Seth. What about you?" he continued. "I haven't met a lot of fae. Do they give you names, or it is something unpronounceably pompous?"

Okay, maybe NOT so friendly.

Ellanden regarded him coldly. "Yes."

By this time, another fight had already started. The arena was oddly practical, staggering matches to give the warriors time to recover in between.

Seth cast a quick glance over his shoulder. "Where are you heading in such a hurry?"

"That's none of your business," Ellanden answered stiffly, just as Freya piped up with a friendly, "We're heading down the western trail."

The others kicked her for silence as the shifter looked up in surprise.

"The western trail—I know it well. Have you any need of a guide?"

There was a quickness to the way he was speaking. An underlying panic Evie hadn't noticed at any point during his fight in the ring. She studied him curiously, looking for any clues.

"And why should we trust you?" she asked. "It's one thing to make jokes in the arena. It's another thing entirely to—"

"I saved your lives," he interrupted.

There was an urgency to the way he was speaking, but his eyes were clear and true.

"If it weren't for me the Red Hand would still be tracking you, haunting your every step. You might be able to outpace them for a while, but eventually they always get what they're after."

A little shiver ran over his shoulders, one he didn't seem aware of himself.

Evie stared at him another moment, then shared a quick glance with her friends.

None of them had ever travelled so far beyond the outer rim, and his talent with a sword would most certainly make him a valuable asset to have on their side. Furthermore, the shifter was right. There *was* that little matter of having saved their lives...

"What experience do you have?" Asher asked quietly, gesturing to the woods. "This part of the realm, you claim to know it well—"

"You cannot be serious," Ellanden interrupted, turning to him in disbelief. "You cannot *possibly* be considering taking this boy along."

Seth pawed the ground impatiently, muttering under his breath. "This *boy* could kick your a—"

"I'd like to see you try!"

"Excellent—tonight, then. When we're camped somewhere far away from here." The shifter glanced quickly back at the roaring crowd before bowing his head in supplication. "...please."

There was a moment of strained silence. The friends looked at each other again then Evie gave Ellanden a little nudge, echoing his own words from before.

"Needs of the majority. It's four to one."

The fae glared at the rest of them, turning that cold gaze to Seth.

"This is a trial run, do you understand? We're taking it day by day."

The shifter lit up with a beaming smile. "Perfect! In that case, we'd better—"

But no sooner had he taken a step towards them than he was jerked back—hands flying up to his throat as if there was some invisible chain wrapped around his neck. His shoulders fell as he glanced at a pair of men standing on the other side of the arena. They began walking his way.

"On second thought...you might have to do that dinner without me."

He waved farewell with a hint of a flush, unwilling to look at any of them directly. The friends found themselves held by dark curiosity, unable to turn away.

"I don't understand," Evie murmured, glancing over his shoulder. "What—"

"My uncle," Seth answered with a tight smile. "You'll know him better as the jackass who tried to rob you in that tavern. Turns out he owed these men some money. When he found out it was me who freed the horses, he decided to kill two birds with one stone. A debt settled for him, and he doesn't have to execute his nephew...win-win."

The men tugged him back again, harder this time.

"Anyway, good luck to you," he said miserably, still trying hard to keep up that smile. "And be careful when you get down to the river. It's a common spot for mercenaries and—"

"What is the debt?" Cosette asked suddenly, speaking for the first time.

The others glanced over in surprise, but none so much as the shifter. "What do you mean?"

"The debt," she repeated sharply, glancing at the men coming up from behind. "What is it?"

Seth shook his head, looking slightly confused. "It's astronomical—"

"Give me a number."

He shook his head, still unable to see what it would matter. "Eighty-five gold pieces."

The men joined them a moment later, smiling politely at the friends while giving the chain none of them could see an unnecessary tug.

"I hope he wasn't bothering you," one of them said conversationally. "You know how these slaves are. Excellent in the ring, but they have trouble letting go of the outside world."

The gang stared back in cold silence. Even the fae had forgotten his quarrel and was glaring back with the darkest kind of hate. Cosette turned to the shifter, staring up into his eyes.

Then all at once, she yanked that chain of white diamonds off her neck.

"Eighty-five gold pieces?" She thrust it into the slaver's hand. "That should cover it."

There was a silent gasp from those people milling around beside them. The slaver's eyes widened incredulously as Seth went very still. When no one spoke, she stepped forward. Fearless.

"Is there a problem? I've just bought this man's freedom. I expected him to be *freed*."

It was suddenly easy to remember that the fae was far more than she was pretending. It was suddenly easy to remember she was the daughter of a warrior princess. The daughter of a dragon.

The man on the left snapped his fingers.

In a flash there was a metallic whisper, then the enchanted chain fell away, not revealing itself until it was lying on the grass. It was a salcor, Evie realized. A wizard's knot. Appearing only when necessary. Capturing only those it was meant to enslave.

Seth's hand lifted slowly, rubbing at his neck.

"Apologies, milady." The slaver inclined his head with a simpering smile, inadvertently using the title she'd grown up hearing all her life. "Is there any other way we might be of service?"

"Yes," she answered coldly, "you can leave the rope here."

The others watched in stunned silence, while Seth carefully lifted his eyes to her face. For a moment it looked like the slaver might actually refuse, then he glanced again at the sparkling gems in his hand and agreed with another instant smile.

"Of course." He coiled it gently and placed it in her hand. "I'd advise you to use caution. A salcor, once knotted, isn't easily undone."

Cosette stuffed it contemptuously into her pocket. "I'm all good without the lesson, thanks."

The men waited in awkward silence, then flinched when she waved them away sharply. They hurried off across the arena, not even bothering with a cursory goodbye as the young fae squared her shoulders and gazed out towards the western trail.

"We should really get moving. There's only a few hours left of daylight, and I for one would like to get as far away from this place as possible before setting up camp."

The others stood in silence as she started moving briskly through the grass. It wasn't until a moment later that she realized no one was following. She paused where she stood, eyes flashing to Ellanden, looking a bit unsure for the first time.

"Don't you agree?"

He stared at her a moment, his eyes glowing with unmistakable pride. "Whatever you think is best."

She flushed, then nodded curtly—continuing her trek through the grass. This time the others followed, leaving only the shifter standing behind.

He hadn't really moved since she took off the necklace. With a wave of dizziness, he realized he hadn't really breathed as well. For a split second he stared after them uncertainly, wondering into what kind of world he'd strayed. Then he pulled in a deep breath and headed after them.

Cosette whirled around the second she heard it, stopping him with just a sweep of her eyes. "What are you doing?"

He froze where he stood, eyes flickering to the pocket that held the rope. "I thought—"

"Only if you like," she interrupted swiftly. "I wasn't joking, what I said before." Their eyes met for a suspended moment before she headed back up the trail. "...you're free."

Chapter 13

When Evie and her friends had first laid eyes on the sprawling settlement, they'd hoped to leave with a bevy of supplies. After surviving that first harrowing night they'd set their sights a bit lower, hoping merely to escape with their lives. That was the extent of it.

Never would they have imagined they'd acquire a new member of the team.

"—higher than average rainfall, so you can imagine what that did to those salmon fishermen coming down the river. They launched a rescue party, but only ever found a few of the boats—"

And a talkative one at that.

For the last few miles Seth had kept up a steady stream of dialogue, halting it with occasional questions and introductions as he tried to figure out who everyone was. The friends didn't make it easy. It had only taken a few basic questions for them to realize what should have been immediately obvious: the shifter was going to recognize their names.

There wasn't a child in the realm who didn't know how the royal children had been abducted from an royal caravan just ten years before. A single catalyzing event, but the world would never be the same. Seth would have been about six or seven at the time. He was going to remember.

Aside from that, there was just the simple conundrum of whether they should share with a virtual stranger the secret of the prophecy, or their nightmarish destination, or their fledgling plan to save the realm before it plunged so far into darkness it was unable to return.

Little things like that.

"—at any rate, my cousin Charlie saw the things with his own eyes, and to this day he swears the puma didn't actually...why did you keep the rope?"

Cosette glanced up in surprise to see him stopped a few feet in front of her. Since leaving the encampment she'd been hiking out in front, but sometime in the midst of one of his endless stories the handsome shifter had slipped into the lead.

"Excuse me?"

"The rope," he repeated intently, staring right at her. "Why did you keep it?"

The fae froze a moment before shaking her head with a puzzled frown. "It was an enchanted rope—able to hold any prisoner until the terms of their capture are met. We're travelling alone through the forest, with limited supplies and no idea when we'll be coming back. We have *no idea* what might be waiting out here for us." She paused ever so slightly. "Did you really think I was going to leave the rope?"

When you put it like that...

The others bit back smiles and Ellanden rolled his eyes, but the shifter had never been so serious. He took a step closer, unconcerned that the rest of them were watching every move.

"So you really don't intend to use it?" he asked quietly, studying her face for even the slightest reaction. "Your business in the arena...it's done?"

Evie's smile faded as the question he *wasn't* asking hung heavy in the air.

Am I still a slave?

The gang immediately sobered as Cosette stared him right in the eyes.

"It's done."

His body tensed as he waited for the rest of it, waited for the other shoe to fall. When nothing happened he was simply bewildered, shaking his head slightly as he tried to understand. "Why would you do that?"

Cosette pulled in a silent breath, trying to think of a suitable response. A child of the castle, she'd been raised to deal with tough situations through either open violence or a passive-aggressive cold war. Simple, direct questions threw her off guard.

Fortunately, this one seemed to have a built-in answer.

"You saved our lives. This makes us square."

There wasn't a person in the forest who didn't think there was more to it. Lucky for the princess, they'd all been raised the same way. All except one.

"Why did you give her back the necklace in the first place?" Freya interjected, ignoring the quiet tension as she stepped up to join them, leaning obliviously against her friend's arm. "And, you know...the other thing."

Cosette's eyes snapped shut a split second as Seth fought back a genuine smile.

"I've always had a weakness for blondes."

...awkward.

"Well, since *that's* all cleared up, I suggest we keep moving." Ellanden swept in between them, deliberately separating everyone at the same time. "Not that your sexual preferences aren't a vital part of whatever happens next."

Cosette blanched in utter mortification, but the shifter only grinned.

"Right you are." He clapped the prince on the shoulder, gazing out over the woods. "Do you want to take the lead, or should I?"

The arm lowered slowly in the silence that followed, but the brazen grin remained.

"My apologies... I mistook that for an invitation."

<hr />

BY THE TIME THE FRIENDS set up camp just a few hours later, a subtle shift in dynamic had taken over the group. None of them noticed it at first. The change was so subtle, they didn't realize what was happening until it was already done. But there was a kind of lightness to the way things were progressing. A sense of positivity that hadn't been there before.

"Heads up!"

There was a flash of silver as a missing tent peg went flying across the campsite, flipping in deadly circles as it whirled through the air. Ellanden glanced up and caught it a second before it could embed itself in the left half of his face.

"Nice reflexes." Seth folded his arms with a grin, watching from the other side of the little clearing. "You know what, there's a chance you might have done okay in the arena after all."

Ellanden straightened up slowly, gripping the peg like he was considering hurling it right back. A look from Asher was enough to stop him. If only for a time.

"Remind me again why we've been graced with your company?" he asked instead, pounding the stake into the ground with unnecessary force. "Is this some kind of penance?"

Seth plopped down beside him, willfully ignoring the fae's blade. "Well, I am a sparkling conversationalist," he said practically. "There's also the fact that I've been an invaluable guide."

"An invaluable guide?" the fae repeated, cratering the peg into the ground. "Down this straight trail we've been walking? You think that's something I couldn't have done myself?"

"...didn't you lead everyone straight into a pack of undead leopards?"

At this point, Asher excused himself (probably to avoid seeing inevitable bloodshed) as the prince straightened up with a scathing glare.

"You have no idea what you're talking about. How were we supposed to know such things roamed the mountain pass? We've only just—"

He caught himself suddenly as Seth lifted his eyebrows, cupping a hand to his ear.

"What's that?" he prompted cheerfully. "You've only just...what?"

The rest of the campsite froze as the fae remained stoically silent, debating what course to take next. There had been no opportunity to discuss what to tell him. Without knowing how long he might be with them, the risk seemed too much to take. But the shifter was turning out to be inconveniently clever. And those sharp eyes of his saw better than most.

"Let's play out a hypothetical," Seth said suddenly, stretching out his long legs. "Here's how *I* think you were going to finish that sentence. 'We've only just...returned to the realm ourselves.'"

Evie's eyes flashed to the others as Ellanden reached discreetly for his blade.

"There's no need to kill me, Your Highness," Seth said quietly, keeping his gaze on the campfire. "After all, we're only playing a little game."

There was a moment of silence. The fae's hand lowered back to his side.

"You travel well, but there are subtle differences about you—things it would be impossible to hide. You get surprised when you shouldn't. The two girls didn't think twice when the Red Hand entered the tavern, but the three of you looked as though you'd never heard of us before. Your clothes are fine, but slightly outdated. Your shoes are old, but hardly used. You still talk about the realm in terms of the five kingdoms, and while I'm all for an abundance of caution it's been hard not to notice how none of you have told me your names. Then, of course, there's always those things you can't hide at all. A vampire, a fae, and a fire-haired shifter. All travelling together."

In the ringing silence that followed, he pushed slowly to his feet.

"You're them, aren't you? The members of the royal family who went missing so long ago."

Evie's every instinct was to deny it. Her every instinct was simply to run. Only a few hours they'd been travelling together, but the man had figured them out so quickly. With echoes of his quiet words ringing in her ears, it seemed to be just a matter of time.

No one would answer. No one would even look at him. But the shifter wasn't the kind to give up. Instead of backing down he walked calmly across the clearing, stopping in front of Cosette.

"Tell me I'm wrong."

Her face paled, but she gave nothing away—breaking his gaze only once to glance over his shoulder at the princess. Evie stared back, rigid with tension, then decided to nod.

"It's true."

The moment shattered as the shifter stepped back with a little gasp, staring at his new companions as if seeing them for the first time. His eyes lingered a moment on each one, trying to connect faces with the stories he'd been told as a child before flying straight back to Cosette.

"So he's your cousin!" he exclaimed in a burst of enlightenment. "The other fae—he's not your boyfriend, he's your cousin!"

Both fae went blank as Evie quickly turned away to hide her smile.

The guy just discovered the missing royal family...and that's all he has to say?

"In that case, it's a pleasure to meet you." He swept back across the clearing, shaking the prince's hand with a winning smile. "I'm sorry for giving you such a hard time earlier. If it's any consolation, I *really* wasn't looking forward to beating you senseless in that ring."

The fae was simply stunned, pulling back his hand a moment later. "You don't..." He trailed off, glancing uncertainly at the others. "You don't have any questions about—"

"Oh, I have plenty of questions," the shifter said cheerfully. "What happened, where have you been, why are you back now? Not the least of which is where the hell we might be going. But I figure those will be answered in due course. For *now*, I'm far more concerned with what we might be having for dinner. I vote venison—who's with me?"

With that, he picked up his sword and headed briskly into the trees—assumedly to slaughter some poor deer the rest of them would eat for dinner. The friends stared after him in a moment of stunned silence before Asher clapped Ellanden's shoulder with a cheerful smile.

"I like him."

"You would," the fae replied.

But in spite of his best efforts, it looked like he was starting to agree.

AS PROMISED, THE FRIENDS feasted on venison that night.

It was more than they'd had in one sitting for a long while, roasted with great care over the fire and seasoned with a number of herbs the shifter had found in the forest. Somewhere in his past, there had been manners involved. The man served everyone a helping before sitting down himself.

"I say you enslave him after all," Ellanden whispered to Cosette, helping himself to another piece. "You still have that rope, and we could use a cook."

"...I'm going to pretend you didn't say that."

The conversations flowed easier and easier as the night went on. Seth turned out to be delightful company, and while the friends weren't exactly forthcoming about their past they had plenty of stories to share from the present. The skeletal leopards were just the latest in a series of misadventures that, when told through the benefit of hindsight, took on a decidedly comical flair.

"—at which point, the giant decided the cousins were married, Ellanden would be allowed to keep his hand after all, and declared Evie was his favorite before taking her out of the cage."

Freya promptly concluded the story, but Seth was on the edge of his seat.

"...*and?*"

The witch glanced up from her food. "Oh—and he forced her to read a book."

The others burst out laughing, while the princess pelted each of them with pinecones.

"Laugh all you want," she chided, "but that was a lot harder than it looked." She returned Seth's questioning stare with a dainty sniff. "There was a great deal of running involved..."

The shifter laughed quietly, throwing another log onto the fire. "You guys have been through it, I'll give you that."

So have you...

Throughout the night, the shifter had listened more than he'd spoken—quietly reveling in the simple companionship he'd been denied for so long. He laughed at all the appropriate times. He contributed some random bit of trivia whenever the conversation circled back to him. But there was a lot more going on beneath the surface. A world of mystery hiding behind those sparkling eyes.

"So your uncle," Ellanden said abruptly, halting the conversation in its tracks, "he gave you over to the settlement right after we fled town?"

Evie stiffened automatically, praying the fae would be kind. But for once, there was no open animosity between them. As he stared across the fire, there was nothing but quiet concern.

The shifter nodded briskly, stoking the embers with the heel of his boot. "We set out for Tarnaq the next morning," he fidgeted involuntarily, wincing at some painful memory, "after he let the rest of the pack have their fun..."

Asher's eyes softened as they found the fading marks on the boy's hands. "Is that where you got those?"

Seth stared at him a moment, then nodded quickly.

The night at the tavern had been the first time he'd actually seen a vampire. When Asher had fed on the deer a few hours earlier, he hadn't been able to tear his eyes away.

"My uncle's idea of a joke." He tried to smile, but for once the skill failed him. "You have the right to defend yourself, but there's only one rule. You're not allowed to shift."

Evie caught her breath, staring across the flames.

She'd seen enough pack exhibitions with her father to imagine what must have happened next. The way the teenager would have been surrounded by a clan of people who were supposed to have been his friends. The way they'd transform, one by one, until the only person left standing was the man in the middle. Then the madness would begin.

From one ring to another.

"Did you try to escape?" she asked softly. "Once they left you in the settlement. Didn't you ever try to get away?"

The shifter was impossibly resourceful for one his age. She couldn't imagine the possibility of such a venture hadn't at least crossed his mind.

He flashed a tight smile, eager to move on to other things. "It's impossible to escape a salcor, and my new guardians kept close tabs on me." His eyes drifted a little farther, resting on Cosette. "If it weren't for this one's addiction to fine jewelry, I'd still be in that arena. They brought out all the worst creatures at night."

A sudden silence fell over the campfire, leaving the others to imagine what that might mean.

"But enough about me," he continued abruptly. "I'm far more interested in what happened to you. Having now met in person, I can't imagine the three of you being dragged away from that caravan by force..."

The princess blushed ever so slightly, exchanging a quick glance with the boys. They'd put it off longer than was reasonable, but there was no delaying the moment any further.

"I received a prophecy," she answered, draping her arms loosely across her knees. "A few nights before we left, there was a festival in the High Kingdom. A feast to celebrate—"

"—the anniversary of the Great War," Seth finished, eyes twinkling with curiosity in the light of the fire. "Every child in the realm was told the story."

She smiled faintly, thinking back to that fateful night. "They only know part of it. They think it started the moment Abel Bishop was poisoned, but in truth the actual story started a ways before..."

For the next half hour, she took their new friend through everything that had happened from the moment the old witch summoned her into the tent. From the words of the prophecy, to her daring gambit to convince the others, to their eventual decision to run away.

At this point, all five of them began watching his reaction very closely.

They say the worst of things are done with the best of intentions. And if there was ever a moment for blame—they wanted to be prepared.

But there was no accusation in Seth's eyes. There was nothing but thoughtful consideration as she took him from place to place. The country to the mine. The witch to the library. Recounting each extraordinary moment, until they'd entered the sorcerer's cave in the middle of a storm.

"At which point, we were put under an enchantment that lasted until Cosette slayed the wizard and freed us from the spell. We've been travelling together ever since."

The forest went quiet. The only sound was the crackling of the logs.

"So this all happened ten years ago," Seth said slowly, trying to piece it together. "Everything you've just said. Except..." He tilted his head curiously, staring at each one. "In your minds, it must feel so much closer."

Freya flashed a quick look at Ellanden, but held her tongue. The prince nodded slowly, reaching down without thinking to take his cousin's hand.

"When Cosette told us how much time had passed, when she told us what had happened in those ten years, I couldn't believe..." His eyes flashed up suddenly, resting on the shifter. "You must know that we never intended—"

Seth held up his hands, shaking his head without judgement. "You did nothing more than was required. I may not know much about prophecies—they don't give them out as freely in the village where I'm from—but I do know your parents saved the realm after reading a few words scribbled out by some kind of prophet. I guess it isn't too much of a stretch to imagine their children might one day be asked to do the same."

From that moment forward, the shifter was part of the group.

To have such a thing absolved by Cosette and Freya was one thing. Both had already pledged themselves to the cause long before they knew what it was. But to hear the words from a total stranger, to have it spoken so plainly...was an invaluable gift.

"The wizard was a piece of bad luck," he admitted. The others laughed quietly, staring into the fire. "So was the basilisk. Although, I don't understand—"

"Actually, we're all waiting for a bit of explanation on that one," Cosette interrupted, eyes flashing between the men as she remembered the vampire's spontaneous apology. "I take it things didn't go well in the tunnel?"

There was a weighted pause, then Asher looked pointedly at his hands.

"Ellanden was helpless and bleeding...and I saved his life."

Seven hells.

Evie let loose another volley of pinecones but the fae only laughed, staring back at his friend with an affectionate smile. "Is that the story we're telling?"

"I think that version of the story would be best."

Freya shook her head with a grin, muttering something that sounded suspiciously like *men*, but Seth had gone suddenly still. Realizing the implications of their story for the first time.

"So this prophecy...that's what you're doing?" he asked quietly, looking from one person to the next. "You're taking the western trail, to get to the...the Dunes?"

Even so long after the battle, he had trouble saying the word. They all did. It was one of those things you learned as children to say in a whispered sort of hush.

Cosette shared a quick glance with the others. "We don't expect you to come," she said softly. Despite having single-handedly ensured the shifter's freedom, the two had yet to really speak. "There's nothing else in the realm that could be so dangerous. The prophecy itself says that not everyone is to return."

He considered this a moment before looking up with a little smile. "But *you're* going."

Their eyes met tentatively across the flames.

Then Ellanden leaned sharply in between them. "Yes, we're *all* going."

The pair looked away quickly, while Asher pulled the fae back with a smile.

"You know," he whispered conspiratorially, "when the guy said he had a thing for blondes, I don't think he meant *you*—"

"Hold your tongue, vampire. Or, rest assured, I'll be telling my version of that story after all."

"So it's decided?" Evie interjected, looking at the shifter curiously. "You'll come?"

He stared a second longer at Cosette, leaning back with a careless grin. "Of course I'll come. Like so many others in my generation, I've been *dying* to see the Dunes for myself. Between that and the promise that some of us won't return?" He gave the woodland princess a roguish wink. "I wouldn't miss it."

Evie stared between them, smothering a secret smile.

This should be interesting...

"Of course," he continued suddenly, "that begs the question of how we're going to get there. I assume you have some kind of plan?"

Ellanden nodded curtly, his former acceptance of the shifter vanishing on a dime. "We're following the river down to the low country. From there, we'll book passage on a ship."

Seth stared back in silence. "...seriously?"

The fae's eyes flashed as he turned to the vampire. "All right, just let me kill him—"

"What's the problem?" Asher interrupted, staring with a frown.

The shifter glanced between them, shaking his head. "Ten years. I keep forgetting—you've been asleep for ten years."

Ellanden ground his teeth together. "Enlighten me."

"Let me put it this way." Seth leaned forward, resting his elbows on his knees. "You guys said you ran into a Carpathian? Where do you think he came from?"

A chill ran up Evie's spine. "You don't mean—"

"They've settled in the low country, took over years ago. The guy you met probably works on one of the ships. They go to Tarnaq often, stocking up on supplies. The only way you're getting across that sea is by their permission, and I guarantee that's not something you're going to get."

Evie's lips parted in dismay, then she turned to Ellanden.

"Is there another way?"

He shook his head, staring with troubled eyes into the fire. "It would take weeks, maybe months. Time we don't have."

The shifter grimaced apologetically and the friends fell silent—each wracking their brains for some kind of solution. After a few minutes, the vampire finally lifted his head.

"Then we'll just have to take one for ourselves."

The others turned to him slowly, and Seth shook his head.

"Take what?" There was a beat of silence. "Wait—take a *ship*?!"

His eyes leapt frantically between them but the friends were already nodding, eyes lighting up with the same reckless smile. Ellanden in particular seemed to think it was a brilliant idea, clapping Asher on the shoulder before turning to Evie with a grin.

"I think we're starting to rub off on him..."

The plan was set, but not everyone was on board.

"You can't be serious," Seth said with a hint of desperation. "You want to *steal* a ship from the Carpathians? I'm as up for adventure as the next guy, but...really? You get this would be the part of the story where somebody dies, right?"

Ellanden flashed a bright smile. "My vote is for the new guy."

The shifter stared incredulously for a moment, then shook his head with a slow smile. "I'd have been better off taking my chances in the ring..."

Chapter 14

For the next five days, the friends travelled without incident through the forest. Considering their previous bout of luck, it was a welcome reprieve. But it wasn't completely coincidental. Their newest member seemed determined to prove his weight in gold.

Having roamed the outskirts of the five kingdoms since he was a child, the shifter knew all the best places to set up camp. He knew all the easy ambush points to stay away from, all the best spots for trapping game and catching fish. At one point, while they were making their way through the forest, he tackled Freya to safety just seconds before she could be tangled in a mercenary's net.

The help was invaluable. And the witch wasn't the only person to agree.

"So how did you learn to do all this?" Evie asked one evening as they gathered around a crackling fire, roasting a pair of squirrels on a long stick.

The shifter had skinned them both in one brisk motion; he'd cleaned them even faster than that. Part of the princess was utterly disgusted. Another part was secretly impressed.

"What do you mean?" Seth lifted his head innocently. "They didn't teach you at the castle?"

It was another thing she liked about him. He could always make her laugh.

"Oh...I bet it was the maids, wasn't it?" he continued knowingly, wiping a bit of grease from his hands. "The ladies-in-waiting. They'd be in charge of things like squirrels."

She nodded seriously, staring back with wide eyes. "Squirrels and mice."

He flashed an automatic grin, which faded almost as quickly. "My dad taught me," he said shortly, laying the stick back over the fire. "When I was first learning to shift, he'd take me into the forest for weeks at a time. Taught me how to look out for the others, provide for myself. I was probably eight or nine. It was heaven."

"You shifted that early?" she asked in surprise. Her father was probably the most famous wolf in the five kingdoms, and even he hadn't managed it until his early teens.

"They say magic sped up a bit in the last few years," he answered with a shrug. "A lot of kids are being born with powers straight away. Makes for an interesting early childhood, I'll tell you that."

She stared into the fire, lost in thought. "I'll bet..."

It had always been said that kids grew up faster in the supernatural community, that powers had a way of maturing you in a way that no amount of parental lecturing ever could. She'd believed it, in theory. She'd always claimed to be quite mature herself. Ten years later, she could only imagine how things had escalated without the magical safeguards the royal army had put in place.

Poverty was rampant, slavery had made a comeback. People of all ages and tribes had been forced to level up if they wanted to survive. Freya was a prime example. Ten years ago, it would have been nearly impossible for a young woman to possess such skill. The princess remembered thinking she would have made a prime student for Petra. Now, she wondered if it was all the same.

"Where is he now?" Asher asked softly. "Your dad."

It was a dangerous question under the best of circumstances. Death was a way of life in the five kingdoms, and if a man was living at the mercy of his uncle it seemed likely his father was no longer around. Sure enough, Seth's eyes tightened before going deliberately clear.

"Dead," he said shortly. "There was a raiding party. I wasn't home."

The vampire bowed his head and the conversation dropped.

It was quiet for a while as the friends passed the sticks of meat back and forth. They had started limiting the use of fire the closer they got to the low country. At this point, they would let it burn just long enough to cook their dinner before stomping it into the dirt.

"I'm surprised you didn't go straight to your own parents," Seth said suddenly. "Once you woke up, I mean. I'm surprised it wasn't your first stop."

There had been good reasons for that.

They were a bit hard to remember now.

"We need to focus on the prophecy," Ellanden replied after a few painful seconds. "Our parents were weeks in the opposite direction, and there just wasn't time. Even if we..." He shook his head, repeating the quiet mantra. "There just wasn't time."

There was no way to think of it without crying, so Evie had resolved to simply not think of it at all. It seemed impossible that she and the others couldn't fire up some kind of flare, send a raven with news of their survival. But any attempt to call attention to themselves would bring attention from the wrong kinds of people. And as Cosette had repeatedly told them, their parents' hideaway was protected with enchantments. No raven could ever make it through.

"We could always find another seeing stone," Asher murmured, as if reading the princess' thoughts. "I know they're rare, but it isn't impossible—"

"Yeah," she nodded quickly, "I know."

Seth watched the exchange with a thoughtful expression, eyes lingering on the vampire's hand resting casually on the princess' knee, before changing the subject with sudden determination.

"In that case, we'll just have to get you back as quickly as possible." He smiled as if it was the easiest thing in the world. "There's no need to venture all the way through the low country; the place is crawling with Carpathians, and we wouldn't make it far. My suggestion is to infiltrate one of the northernmost docks. Get in and out before anyone is the wiser…"

He trailed off with an odd expression, lifting his face to the wind. Both fae had frozen with the same worried frown. The vampire was already standing—fangs sinking slowly into his lip as he silently pulled Evie to her feet.

"What is it?" she whispered, eternally frustrated that her famed 'shifter senses' had yet to make an appearance. "What do you hear?"

He opened his mouth to answer, then turned his face instead—staring with sudden attention at an outcropping of rocks deep within the forest. One hand lifted slightly in the air but Ellanden and Seth were already moving, silently moving forward with a bow and a sword.

"Put out the fire," Asher murmured under his breath.

Freya hurried to do as he asked, sweeping a mountain of dirt over the smoldering logs then pushing to her feet, pale and shaken.

Considering the state of most travelers who ventured through the woods, the six friends were far more capable than most. Two fae, two shifters, a vampire, and a witch. Not to mention their training. Not to mention that they were armed. But they'd wandered into the territory of the Carpathians, and Carpathians weren't your average opponents. If there was ever a time to be afraid…

"How many?" Evie whispered, lifting her bow from the ground. "Can you tell?"

Ellanden listened a moment, then shook his head.

"More than ten, fewer than twenty." His head tilted with the hint of a frown. "It's difficult to say one way or another. There's a chance they haven't even—"

A wild shout broke through the trees.

"—seen us."

There was no time to prepare. There was no time to consider another option. A half-formed thought flashed through Evie's mind, wondering if she should use the bow or try to shift instead. But then the ferns parted and the enemy was upon them.

There was a chorus of shouts, followed by a clang of metal as the two groups crashed together in the middle of the trees. Showers of neon sparks exploded from one end of the clearing to another. Arrows flashed through the air with deadly accuracy and speed. Before long, the ground beneath them was stained with splashes of blood.

And still, the Carpathians kept coming.

Evie let loose another arrow, then surveyed the clearing with a breathless gasp. She understood now why the others had been having such difficulty pinning down exact location and numbers. Carpathian soldiers were flying in from both sides—dropping bloody bags of game before drawing their weapons and charging into the fray. It seemed their luck hadn't held after all. They'd unintentionally set up camp directly in the path of a hunting party on their way back home.

If you can call it that...

It didn't matter how many rushed through the trees, Evie didn't think she would ever get used to the sight of them. It was shocking every time. Standing a head taller than the tallest man she knew, each one looked strong enough to single-handedly tear down one of the towering redwoods in a fit of rage. And rage they could. Never before had the princess seen such violent delight as they swept towards the group of teenagers, determined to tear them limb from limb.

That being said, the friends were all still standing. At least for now.

Ellanden thrust an arrow into the neck of a soldier before fitting it to the bow to take down two others. Freya was backed into a corner, but with streams of liquid light dripping from her hands none of the men pressing her wanted to get too close. A stack of bodies had already piled up around Asher's feet and Cosette was firing down arrows like a sniper, perched halfway up one of the towering trees.

A surge of relief rushed through the princess before she realized, with a sudden stab of guilt, that she'd completely forgotten about the newest member of their fellowship.

...and the guy was having a hard time.

Seth had been standing closest when the horde surged through the trees and was instantly overrun, doing his best to hold them off with nothing more than a dented sword. To make matters worse, some of the Carpathians clearly recognized him from the gladiatorial arena and were thrilled at the chance to fight against him themselves. Already, about a dozen had formed a tight-knit circle around him—isolating him from the others as they rushed in two at a time to attack.

"Landi!" the princess screamed, directing his attention to the far side of the clearing.

The fae saw the circle and quickly fired off three rounds, but he was running out of arrows and more soldiers were charging in from the trees. Cosette had already used up everything in her quiver and was being forced to rejoin the others on the forest floor, fighting with a pair of knives.

As for the rest of them, they were too consumed with their own battles to notice much of anything else happening amongst the trees. Short on hands, Freya had bewitched a knife to fight alongside her. It hovered in the air above her shoulder, darting in without warning to attack. Asher was in a similar state, flitting like a ghost from person to person, reappearing for only a moment after each one, streams of blood dripping from his fangs.

With every second that passed, Seth was running out of time.

The princess couldn't see much of what was happening, but she could hear it all just fine. A chorus of dark laughter rang out with every fresh attack, followed by the frantic clash of metal on metal and a series of muffled cries. She had been isolated several yards away, but the rest of them were fighting in their separate corners. There was no one else who could possibly get to him in time.

Please let this work...

In a burst of determination, Evie flung her emerald cloak to the ground. Her shoes were soon to follow. Already, her body was beginning to change shape. The forest blurred for a split second, then sharpened into sudden focus as the girl vanished and a crimson wolf sprang up in her place. It landed lightly upon the forest floor, a blistering growl ripping out of its chest.

"You're a shifter?!"

She took one look at the stunned soldier in front of her then leapt straight into the air, knocking the sword from his hand and coming down hard on his chest. At least, she tried. Most people would have fallen, but Carpathians weren't most people. This one simply took a step back for balance before grabbing her with both hands.

That's when the fighting really began.

Seven hells!

A flash of pain shot through her body as he struck her repeatedly with those massive fists, trying his best to dislodge her vicious claws. Her legs buckled, and when one of the punches grazed the side of her face the world around her flickered dangerously dark. But the wolves of Belaria were feared for a reason. Before the man could draw a second weapon pure animalistic instinct took over, and she sank her teeth deep into the curve of his neck.

...gross.

Even governed by the feral instincts of a wolf, she couldn't help but be disgusted. A burst of blood exploded in her mouth, trickling down her throat even as she forbid herself to swallow. With a frenzied cry she shook her head back and forth, trying to finish the job, then leapt quickly to the ground once more as the barrel-chested warrior finally collapsed to the ground.

How does Asher drink this?!

She pawed miserably at her face, trying to collect her senses before retching uncontrollably onto the ground. Across the clearing, the vampire glanced up in alarm at the sound. His face stilled for a second in confusion, then she could have sworn he rolled his eyes.

She flashed him an apologetic look, darting across the forest floor.

Ironically enough, from lower down she had a better view of what was happening. Through the legs of the surrounding Carpathians, she saw that Seth had dropped to one knee. His sword was still flashing as he fought them back, but there were large gashes ripped over the majority of his body and the guy was losing a crazy amount of blood.

"Drop the sword," one of the soldiers taunted, unconcerned with his countrymen dropping dead in the forest behind. "We'll take you back to the arena. It was a thrill watching you fight."

Another rushed towards him, slicing the length of his collarbone before being driven back.

"Nah, I say we finish him right here. The kid took down a wendigo all by himself. I lost a lot of money on that fight." He drew a knife, running it along his tongue. "A *lot* of money..."

There was another slash of a knife and Seth fell to the ground with a soft cry. The air around him shimmered, but steadied when he got a swift kick to the ribs. Whatever grisly demise the mob of Carpathians was planning, it was clear they wanted him to face it as a man.

And here I'd rather see the wolf...

Without a thought to her own safety Evie streaked across the clearing, vaulting straight over the heads of the brutish soldiers to land beside Seth in the circle. The chorus of laughter came to a sudden stop as she lowered her head to the ground, glaring up at them with a savage growl.

New blades were drawn. The game had just gotten serious.

Are you okay?

She couldn't ask the question aloud, but from the second she landed it became clear that Seth was in even worse shape than she thought. His skin was shredded, his bones were cracked, and every gasping breath sounded like it could be his last.

He'd thrown up his hand instinctively when she landed beside him, thinking her to be some new threat, then crumpled to the ground in sheer exhaustion when he realized who she was.

Their eyes met for just an instant and he panted the quiet words.

"I need to shift."

She nodded her head.

I can help with that.

Before the Carpathians had a chance to coordinate an attack she launched one of her own, springing from person to person in such a blur of speed they were forced to stumble back. Blades flashed as they tried to spear her, but by the time they'd taken the swing she'd already moved on to the next person, running so fast her feet barely touched the forest floor.

It would be impossible to take on so many by herself. She had no delusion that she could fend them off for long. But her friends were already fighting their way closer. And, more importantly, her reckless diversion had given Seth all the time he'd need—

In a flash, another wolf sprang up beside her. This one was a deep brown, like rich molasses, with amber tints strewn through his glossy fur. He was bigger than she was. Taller, too. But still lean and light on his feet. And while he might have been dripping a river of blood, there was a look in his eyes that made the princess eternally grateful they happened to be fighting on the same side.

They didn't wait for the others. They charged headfirst into the fray.

All her life, Evie had seen wolves fighting together. The Belarian princess might not have shifted yet herself, but since the day of her birth she'd been a treasured member of the pack. She remembered watching them train from the balcony of the castle, marveling at the breathless speed, the instinctual synchronicity as warriors from all over the kingdom came together as one.

All her life, she'd seen it. But she'd never gotten to participate until that day.

"EVIE!"

Ellanden sprinted towards her, then stopped when he saw the two wolves fighting, taking a moment to catch his breath as they lunged together at the Carpathian horde. One would go low, the other would jump high. One would attack, the other would defend. And that was just when he could see them. Most of the time, they were mere streaks of color before his eyes.

"Never mind. You...you got it."

Never had the princess felt such a thing. It was like they'd rehearsed it. Each move was so deeply ingrained, it was as if she'd been doing it her entire life. The ground felt cool and natural beneath her paws. Each muscle tensed and coiled as if she'd been born to take flight.

In the distance, she heard her friends shouting. In her periphery, she vaguely noted that the rest of the hunting party was lying dead on the ground. She should have cared more. She should have noticed that of the twelve soldiers she and Seth had been fighting, only one remained.

But she didn't. And she didn't ever want to shift back.

There was a whispering of fur as Seth pulled himself away from the man he'd been fighting and landed on the ground by her side. In an animalistic gesture, the two knocked heads before they turned as one to the Carpathian remaining—the one who'd offered to return him to the ring.

A low growl started deep in his chest and she took a step back. She'd killed plenty of her own. This one was for him.

It was over before she knew it.

Just a streak of fur, followed by a tortured scream. That scream cut off in a gurgle. When Seth lifted his head a moment later, there were streams of blood dripping down his chin.

Their eyes met in the silence that followed. Evie could have sworn he smiled.

Then, suddenly...he was a wolf no longer.

She skittered back a few steps, blinking in disorientation as the wolf vanished and a handsome man stood up in its place. He was naked and bloody, but they weren't far from where he'd dropped his cloak. In a graceful movement, he knelt and secured it over his shoulders. Then he straightened up and turned back to her with a beaming smile.

"Not bad, Princess."

She stared at him a moment longer, the twin natures warring for dominance in her mind. Then she pulled in a deep breath and stood up beside him, shaking out her long, wavy hair.

"You weren't so bad yourself. *After* I saved you."

Instead of arguing he threw back his head with a laugh, lifting a bracing hand to the side of his ribs. "Yeah, well...I guess that happens sometimes."

The casual laughter caught her off guard. As did the casual return to two legs. He was shaking leaves from his hair, acting as though such a thing happened all the time. But her mind was still trapped in the wolf, replaying with relish each screaming kill that had fallen to the forest floor.

She was still grinning, still trying to come down from the high, when a pair of cool hands draped a cloak over her shoulders. She startled in surprise then turned around to see Asher standing behind her, staring down with a secret little smile.

"Embracing our inner animal, are we?" His eyes twinkled before flickering across the clearing to a little pool of blood. "I see you had no interest in embracing mine."

At first, she didn't know what he was talking about. Then her face screwed up in horror.

"Ash, I didn't mean to offend you or anything, but...holy crap! A mouthful of *blood*? How can you drink that stuff? I couldn't even swallow!"

He laughed again, stroking back a lock of fiery hair. "I guess it's an acquired taste..."

She stilled suddenly, noticing the fangs for the first time. It was strange how natural the sight of them had become. Before they'd left the castle, the vampire had liked to pretend they didn't exist.

"I see you did well," she said cautiously, wondering if he'd actually fed.

His smiled faded for a split second, then he fixed it carefully back on his face. "Good thing that sorcerer didn't take them. Sometimes they're more useful than a blade."

She grinned up at him, taking his hand, when a frantic girl pushed through.

"Are you all right?!"

Cosette rushed past them both, sliding to a stop in front of Seth. Her face was bloody and her knuckles were violently bruised, but in those bright eternal eyes there was nothing but concern.

"I tried to get over here, but they had me pinned down," she murmured, avoiding his gaze whilst assessing his injuries as best she could. "I think some of these ribs are definitely broken—"

He pressed a finger to her lips, staring down with a tender smile. "Seven hells you're beautiful."

She froze in shock, staring up at him. "I...I don't—"

"Actually, you're kind of a mess," Freya interjected, skipping lightly to her side. "Not to freak you out or anything, but I'm pretty sure there are entrails in your hair."

Cosette was still lifting her hand in horror when Ellanden pushed swiftly between them, making a silent assessment of each of the friends to make sure they were all right. The prince himself looked like he'd been through the wringer—with a dislocated shoulder and a pair of savage scratches running up the side of his face. But he was still standing. And he clearly had a plan what to do next.

"That ship we need...? We should get it *right now*."

Evie blinked in surprise, thinking they'd done quite enough for one day. "Are you serious? Ellanden, we're lucky to have made it out of this with our lives—"

"That's exactly the point," he interrupted. "We're the only ones still standing. Not a single Carpathian who went out hunting is going to be coming back. How long do you think it'll be before the rest of the horde sends people out looking for them? How long before all ships are grounded? Before there's extra security on the docks?"

"He's right," Asher murmured, though he didn't look happy about it. "If there's even a slight chance of us pulling this thing off, we'll have to do it right now."

"Seth, how close are we to the nearest settlement?"

The wolf tried to answer, but his eyes were on something else. "...hmm?"

"The settlement." Ellanden snapped his fingers in front of him. "How far?"

Seth nodded quickly. "Oh, right. It's, uh...it's just over the..."

A strange look settled over him as he pointed to a strange-looking pile by the trees. It took Evie a second to figure out they were bodies. Or they had been...at some point.

The shifter grimaced involuntarily, fighting the urge to step back. "What happened to those guys?"

Ellanden followed his gaze impatiently, then found himself grimacing as well. "Freya, uh...melted them."

The friends turned as one to stare at the little witch, and Seth nodded again.

"...oh."

There was a beat of awkward silence.

"The settlement," the shifter repeated, recovering quickly. "It's just a few miles away, down in the base of the valley. There's a port on the western side. If we hurry—"

"—if we hurry, we should be able to get there before anyone knows the hunting party is gone," Ellanden finished with a slow smile. "How about it, guys? You up for it?"

They certainly didn't look it. Between the six of them, there weren't many parts that hadn't been smeared with a generous helping of blood. Muscles were bruised, clothes were torn, and whatever stores of energy they had after a day of hiking had been completely used up.

But the looks on their faces told a different story entirely.

"Are we up for it?" Evie repeated. "Are we up for sneaking into a Carpathian settlement in the middle of the night?"

"After slaughtering one of their hunting parties," Cosette added practically.

Freya twiddled her fingers with a blush. "And maybe melting them a little bit..."

"All to steal a ship that we can sail to the Dunes?" Seth inserted with a grin. "A ship that I assume is going to be heavily guarded."

"So that we can find a powerful magical relic to restore the kingdoms and drive the shadow of darkness from the land?" Asher concluded.

"Are we *up* for it?"

A little grin crept up the side of Evie's face.

"Absolutely."

THE END

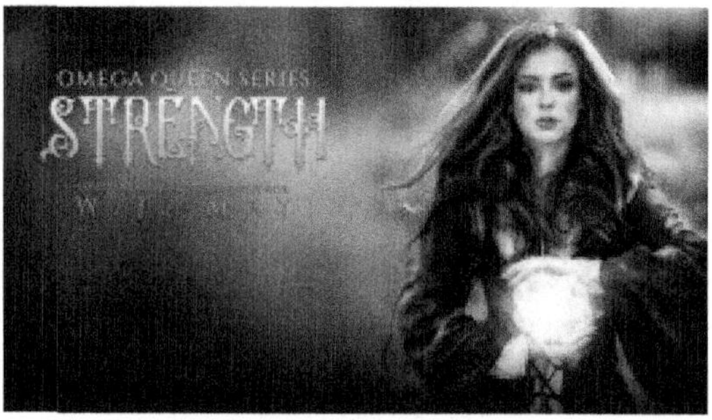
OMEGA QUEEN SERIES
STRENGTH

STRENGTH Book #5 Blurb

TIME IS RUNNING OUT.

As an insidious darkness sweeps across the land, Evie and her friends find themselves in a race to fulfill the prophecy. They acquire a ship and make haste for the Dunes. But, as usual, fate has other plans...

Instead of arriving at their destination, the friends find themselves stranded on the shores of a distant land. A land where the rules don't matter and nothing is as it seems. In the quest to band together, powers are tested and relationships are strained. No matter how hard they try to move forward, it always seems like they're falling several steps behind.

A change is coming, but can the friends rise to meet the challenge? Will they find the stone and stop the darkness in time? Or do Evie's dreams tell a fateful warning...and they're already too late?

The Queen's Alpha Series

Eternal
Everlasting
Unceasing
Evermore
Forever
Boundless
Prophecy
Protected
Foretelling
Revelation
Betrayal
Resolved

The Omega Queen Series

Discipline
Bravery
Courage
Conquer
Strength
Validation
Approval
Blessing
Balance
Grievance
Enchanted
Gratified

Find W.J. May

Website:
http://www.wjmaybooks.com
Facebook:
https://www.facebook.com/pages/Author-WJ-May-FAN-PAGE/141170442608149
Newsletter:
SIGN UP FOR W.J. May's Newsletter to find out about new releases, updates, cover reveals and even freebies!
http://eepurl.com/97aYf

More books by W.J. May

The Chronicles of Kerrigan

BOOK I - *Rae of Hope* is **FREE!**
Book Trailer:
http://www.youtube.com/watch?v=gILAwXxx8MU
Book II - *Dark Nebula*
Book Trailer:
http://www.youtube.com/watch?v=Ca24STi_bFM
Book III - *House of Cards*
Book IV - *Royal Tea*
Book V - *Under Fire*
Book VI - *End in Sight*
Book VII – *Hidden Darkness*
Book VIII – *Twisted Together*
Book IX – *Mark of Fate*
Book X – *Strength & Power*
Book XI – *Last One Standing*
BOOK XII – *Rae of Light*

PREQUEL –
Christmas Before the Magic
Question the Darkness
Into the Darkness
Fight the Darkness
Alone the Darkness
Lost the Darkness

SEQUEL –
   Matter of Time
   Time Piece
   Second Chance
   Glitch in Time
   Our Time
   Precious Time

Hidden Secrets Saga:
Download Seventh Mark part 1 For FREE
Book Trailer:
http://www.youtube.com/watch?v=Y-_vVYC1gvo

Like most teenagers, Rouge is trying to figure out who she is and what she wants to be. With little knowledge about her past, she has questions but has never tried to find the answers. Everything changes when she befriends a strangely intoxicating family. Siblings Grace and Michael, appear to have secrets which seem connected to Rouge. Her hunch is confirmed when a horrible incident occurs at an outdoor party. Rouge may be the only one who can find the answer.

An ancient journal, a Sioghra necklace and a special mark force life-altering decisions for a girl who grew up unprepared to fight for her life or others.

All secrets have a cost and Rouge's determination to find the truth can only lead to trouble...or something even more sinister.

RADIUM HALOS - THE SENSELESS SERIES
Book 1 is FREE

Everyone needs to be a hero at one point in their life.

The small town of Elliot Lake will never be the same again.

Caught in a sudden thunderstorm, Zoe, a high school senior from Elliot Lake, and five of her friends take shelter in an abandoned uranium mine. Over the next few days, Zoe's hearing sharpens drastically, beyond what any normal human being can detect. She tells her friends, only to learn that four others have an increased sense as well. Only Kieran, the new boy from Scotland, isn't affected.

Fashioning themselves into superheroes, the group tries to stop the strange occurrences happening in their little town. Muggings, break-ins, disappearances, and murder begin to hit too close to home. It leads the team to think someone knows about their secret - someone who wants them all dead.

An incredulous group of heroes. A traitor in the midst. Some dreams are written in blood.

Courage Runs Red
The Blood Red Series
Book 1 is FREE

WHAT IF COURAGE WAS your only option?

When Kallie lands a college interview with the city's new hot-shot police officer, she has no idea everything in her life is about to change. The detective is young, handsome and seems to have an unnatural ability to stop the increasing local crime rate. Detective Liam's particular interest in Kallie sends her heart and head stumbling over each other.

When a raging blood feud between vampires spills into her home, Kallie gets caught in the middle. Torn between love and family loyalty she must find the courage to fight what she fears the most and possibly risk everything, even if it means dying for those she loves.

Daughter of Darkness - Victoria
Only Death Could Stop Her Now
The Daughters of Darkness is a series of female heroines who may or may not know each other, but all have the same father, Vlad Montour. Victoria is a Hunter Vampire

HUNTRESS SERIES
USA TODAY BESTSELLING AUTHOR
W.J. MAY
LOOK BACK
MASTER
PERMISSION

PROPHECY SERIES
USA TODAY BESTSELLING AUTHOR
• W.J. MAY •
PROPHECY
• W.J. MAY •
PROPHECY
• W.J. MAY •
PROPHECY
• W.J. MAY •

The Chronicles of
KERRIGAN
W.J. May
RAE OF HOPE
DARK NEBULA
HOUSE OF CARDS
ROYAL TEA
UNDER FIRE
END IN SIGHT

THE HIDDEN SECRETS SAGA
W.J. MAY

Don't miss out!

Visit the website below and you can sign up to receive emails whenever W.J. May publishes a new book. There's no charge and no obligation.

https://books2read.com/r/B-A-SSF-MDXDB

BOOKS 2 READ

Connecting independent readers to independent writers.

Did you love *Conquer*? Then you should read *The Price For Peace*[1] by W.J. May!

How do you keep fighting when you've already been claimed?

When sixteen-year-old Elise is ripped from her home and taken to the royal palace as a permanent 'guest', she thinks her life is over.

Little does she know it has only just begun...

After befriending a group of other captives, including the headstrong Will, Elise finds herself swept away to a world she never knew existed—polished, sculpted, and refined until she can hardly recognize her own reflection. She should be happy to have escaped the poverty of her former life. But she knows a dark truth.

The palace is a dream on the surface, but a nightmare underneath.

---

1. https://books2read.com/u/38EZXr

2. https://books2read.com/u/38EZXr

With a dwindling population, the royals have imprisoned the teenagers to marry and breed. Only seven days remain of freedom before they will be selected by a courtier and forever claimed.

Danger lurks around every corner. The only chance of escape is death.

But when the day of the claiming finally arrives...the world will never be the same.

Royal Factions

The Price for Peace – Book 1

The Cost for Surviving – Book 2

The Punishment for Deception – Book 3

Faking Perfection – Book 4

The Most Cherished – Book 5

The Strength to Endure – Book 6

Read more at www.wjmaybooks.com.

Also by W.J. May

Bit-Lit Series
Lost Vampire
Cost of Blood
Price of Death

Blood Red Series
Courage Runs Red
The Night Watch
Marked by Courage
Forever Night
The Other Side of Fear
Blood Red Box Set Books #1-5

Daughters of Darkness: Victoria's Journey
Victoria
Huntress
Coveted (A Vampire & Paranormal Romance)
Twisted
Daughter of Darkness - Victoria - Box Set

Great Temptation Series
The Devil's Footsteps
Heaven's Command
Mortals Surrender

Hidden Secrets Saga
Seventh Mark - Part 1
Seventh Mark - Part 2
Marked By Destiny
Compelled
Fate's Intervention
Chosen Three
The Hidden Secrets Saga: The Complete Series

Kerrigan Chronicles
Stopping Time
A Passage of Time
Ticking Clock
Secrets in Time
Time in the City
Ultimate Future

Mending Magic Series
Lost Souls
Illusion of Power
Challenging the Dark

Castle of Power
Limits of Magic
Protectors of Light

Omega Queen Series
Discipline
Bravery
Courage
Conquer

Paranormal Huntress Series
Never Look Back
Coven Master
Alpha's Permission
Blood Bonding
Oracle of Nightmares
Shadows in the Night
Paranormal Huntress BOX SET #1-3

Prophecy Series
Only the Beginning
White Winter
Secrets of Destiny

Royal Factions
The Price For Peace

The Cost for Surviving

The Chronicles of Kerrigan
Rae of Hope
Dark Nebula
House of Cards
Royal Tea
Under Fire
End in Sight
Hidden Darkness
Twisted Together
Mark of Fate
Strength & Power
Last One Standing
Rae of Light
The Chronicles of Kerrigan Box Set Books # 1 - 6

The Chronicles of Kerrigan: Gabriel
Living in the Past
Present For Today
Staring at the Future

The Chronicles of Kerrigan Prequel
Christmas Before the Magic
Question the Darkness
Into the Darkness
Fight the Darkness
Alone in the Darkness

Lost in Darkness
The Chronicles of Kerrigan Prequel Series Books #1-3

The Chronicles of Kerrigan Sequel
A Matter of Time
Time Piece
Second Chance
Glitch in Time
Our Time
Precious Time

The Hidden Secrets Saga
Seventh Mark (part 1 & 2)

The Kerrigan Kids
School of Potential
Myths & Magic
Kith & Kin
Playing With Power

The Queen's Alpha Series
Eternal
Everlasting
Unceasing
Evermore
Forever

Boundless
Prophecy
Protected
Foretelling
Revelation
Betrayal
Resolved

The Senseless Series
Radium Halos - Part 1
Radium Halos - Part 2
Nonsense
Perception
The Senseless - Box Set Books #1-4

Standalone
Shadow of Doubt (Part 1 & 2)
Five Shades of Fantasy
Zwarte Nevel
Shadow of Doubt - Part 1
Shadow of Doubt - Part 2
Four and a Half Shades of Fantasy
Dream Fighter
What Creeps in the Night
Forest of the Forbidden
Arcane Forest: A Fantasy Anthology
The First Fantasy Box Set

Watch for more at www.wjmaybooks.com.

About the Author

About W.J. May

Welcome to USA TODAY BESTSELLING author W.J. May's Page! SIGN UP for W.J. May's Newsletter to find out about new releases, updates, cover reveals and even freebies! http://eepurl.com/97aYf

Website: http://www.wjmaybooks.com

Facebook: http://www.facebook.com/pages/Author-WJ-May-FAN-PAGE/141170442608149?ref=hl *Please feel free to connect with me and share your comments. I love connecting with my readers.*

W.J. May grew up in the fruit belt of Ontario. Crazy-happy childhood, she always has had a vivid imagination and loads of energy. After her father passed away in 2008, from a six-year battle with cancer (which she still believes he won the fight against), she began to write again. A passion she'd loved for years, but realized life was too short to keep putting it off. She is a writer of Young Adult, Fantasy Fiction and where ever else her little muses take her.

Read more at www.wjmaybooks.com.

Printed in Great Britain
by Amazon